A Y.N'S MUSE FOR THE SUMMER

NAI

STAY UP TO DATE

To stay up to date on new releases, plus get information on contests, sneak peeks and more,

Click the link below...
https://mailchi.mp/6d21003686d1/subscribe

SOUNDTRACKS

Scan the QR Code below to listen to the Soundtracks/Singles of some of your favorite U.A.D titles:

Don't have Spotify or Apple Music?
No Sweat!
Visit your choice streaming platform and search URBAN AINT DEAD.

Currently on lock serving a bid?
JPay, iHeartRadio, WHATEVER!
We got you covered.
Simply log into your facility's kiosk or tablet, go to music and
search URBAN AINT DEAD.

U.A.D PRESENTS

Like & Follow us on social media:

FB - URBAN AINT DEAD

IG: @uadpresents

Tik Tok - @uadpresents

Submission Guidelines

Submit the first three chapters of your completed manuscript to urbanaintdead@gmail.com, subject line: Your book's title. The manuscript must be in a .doc file and sent as an attachment. The document should be in Times New Roman, double-spaced, and in size 12 font. Also, provide your synopsis and full contact information. If sending multiple submissions, they must each be in a separate email. Have a story but no way to submit it electronically? You can still submit to URBAN AINT DEAD. Send in the first three chapters, written or typed, of your completed manuscript to:

URBAN AINT DEAD
P.O Box 448
Maybrook, NY 12543

DO NOT send original manuscript. Must be a duplicate.
Provide your synopsis and a cover letter containing your full contact information.
Thanks for considering URBAN AINT DEAD.

A NOTE FROM THE AUTHOR

Ay… before we get started, I'm telling y'all right damn now.
THIS IS A NOVELLA. A good ass NOVELLA. But a NOVELLA
nonetheless. If you read fast, read slow.
I DON'T WANNA ARGUE!

1

———

AMARIYAH

*I*f someone would've told me two years ago that I'd be sitting here eight and a half months pregnant, watching the man I once loved pack his stuff to move out, I would've called them crazy. But right now, in this moment, the only person crazy was Jalen for thinking I was about to stay in this dead-end relationship for the sake of our child. I didn't come from a line of women that stuck around and loved a man through it all. I could love you through a lot, but through it all and no ring, that was where you lost me. Being with Jalen was starting to require too much brain power. A bitch could barely remember where I put my damn keys since being pregnant. I didn't have the mental capacity to continue dealing with his bullshit too.

I no longer clung to the hope that things could or would get better. Not only did Jalen want to live life as a single man in a relationship, but he also wanted to live life as a single, **complacent** man in a relationship. And that was where I drew the goddamn line. Jalen didn't want to grow. He wanted to make plans with no execution. In other words, he liked to talk a good game, but when it was time to do, he had every excuse to not. I refused to be around that kind of energy any longer.

"You gon' sit here and watch me the whole time? Like a nigga tryna take something that don't belong to me or sum'n. Don't you have to work today?"

I glanced up from my Kindle and shook my head. I just knew he wasn't going to pack peacefully. He wanted a fight out of me. However, I was on to him. A fight with Jalen would indicate that there was still something there. He lived for a back-and-forth with me, yet another thing I'd come to dislike about him. Because what I look like trying to out argue a man?

Shifting in my bed, I winced a little from the pressure in my lower back. "I'm not watching you, and I'm officially on maternity leave as of today." My tone was non-confrontational, but the hint of *don't fuck with me today* was evident.

The baby had dropped, making sleeping more uncomfortable and me more irritable. I was ready to evict her from my womb just as fast as I was evicting her daddy from my house. I had every intention on working up until the week before my due date, but baby girl wasn't having it, and neither was my staff or clients. My grandmother even had to threaten me to sit down. This time around, I listened to my body.

"This shit crazy." He continued on like I knew he would. "So, now you're choosing to be a single mother rather than to work things out for the sake of the child we planned? What happened to raising our daughter together?"

"What we agreed to was raising our daughter in a loving and healthy environment. We don't have to be in the same household to do so. And you and I both know that we haven't been on the same page in some time. I'd rather end it here than to use our child as the one thing that keeps us together."

Setting my Kindle down, I swung my feet over the bed and pushed myself up from it. Amari had started to two step on my bladder, and I had to rush to the bathroom before I peed on myself. In my haste, I didn't close the door, leaving an opening for Jalen to stand in the doorway and watch me.

"Mari, man. Once I'm gone, I'm gone. This ain't gon' be me leaving for a few nights for you to get your mind right. Real shit."

"When you're gone, you're gone," I repeated, nodding. "Is this your way of telling me you're not interested in being a parent if we're not together? Cause if that's the case, make it plain for me so I can move accordingly."

Getting up from the toilet, I washed my hands and leaned against the sink, as I dried them. He froze for a few seconds, likely getting his thoughts together. I remained quiet, as I stared at him hard, hoping that he chose his words carefully.

"I'm saying I won't be doing the back-and-forth."

"We're on the same page with that. The question I asked was regarding your parenting."

"I mean, shit," he shrugged, "I'm gonna be here so long as you let me."

The silence that came after his statement was heavy – heavy because, for the first time, I felt absolutely nothing for the man that stood before me. This wasn't the man who had promised me and our unborn child the world, no matter what. Right now, Jalen was a boy who thought holding his presence over my child's head was going to somehow get me to change my mind about us. He was sadly mistaken.

Digesting his lame ass encrypted response, I nodded my own. "Do me a favor and be gone by the time I get out the shower. And please take **everything** that belongs to you, down to the dirty clothes you have in the laundry room."

"Remember this moment," he said in a low, bitter tone. "This was your doing," he added, sounding all dramatic.

"Trust. This is a moment I **won't** forget." I closed the door on him physically and mentally.

I knew I was stepping into a new chapter, and Jalen had

made it clear what he was and wasn't going to do in not so many words. Turning on the shower, I stripped out of my pajamas and admired my belly in the mirror. It glowed in the light from the shea butter I applied every night to keep moisturized and avoid stretch marks as best I could. My grandmother got a kick out of that every time I said it. Her reply would always be, "Mari, those scars show you been through some shit. You bout to be a mother, baby. Embrace it."

Smiling, I rubbed my belly and felt a kick to my side. "Good morning to you too, Happy Feet. I know you probably heard that misunderstanding between me and your dad but trust me when I say Mommy is gonna make sure you don't come into a world of dysfunction. It's you above any and everything, my girl."

My breakup with Jalen didn't make me sad. I'd seen it coming. If anything, I felt relieved – relieved from the burden of a relationship I knew no longer served me.

When I got out the shower, Jalen was gone, along with his belongings, as I'd requested. I was glad he bowed out gracefully. It avoided a phone call that would get him removed from the earth permanently. With my robe open, showing all belly and soft, glistening skin, I waddled over to my closet to grab something to wear for the day. I needed to get out and get some air, so my plan was to grab a few things from the grocery store for my grandmother and hang out with her for part of the day. I didn't bother calling to let her know I was coming or to ask if she needed anything because knowing her, she was good for saying she had her necessities and didn't want anyone shopping for her.

Grandma Nita was my dad's mom and the dopest grandmother ever. She'd raised me from the age of sixteen after my mother was killed in a shootout as she walked out of a store around the corner from my grandmother's building. The sun hadn't set before my father found the shooter and killed him in front of a crowd – right outside of that same store. I lost two parts of me that very day, my mother to the grave and my father to the penal system. Some didn't understand and even questioned why a man as poised as Princeton Baker, who had a name that rang far beyond the streets of New York, would move in such an emotional manner, especially for his ex-wife who he'd been divorced from for years.

I always said they didn't know **true love**. And they damn sure didn't know my father. Princeton Baker loved my mother, Marilyn, hard when they were together and even harder after the divorce. There was no doubt in my mind that someone was dying behind her that night. My father moved on principle, loyalty, and love immediately after. Between the two of them, I had the perfect balance – my mother's heart and my father's mind. The lessons and morals they instilled in me made me a well-rounded woman.

Pulling a pair of maternity biker shorts from my dresser drawer, I paired them with a cropped, white button up that tied under my breasts. It gave my bump a peek-a-boo moment but not too much. Even pregnant, I made sure to remain the fashion forward girly that I was before my belly became my everyday accessory. The bump didn't stop my style. If anything, it enhanced it.

Releasing my hair from the silk scarf, I brushed through the jet-black tresses. The tape-ins I had put in were laid to perfection down to the middle of my back. You couldn't tell a bad bitch nothing when her hair was done. **I was that bad bitch.** Adding a few gold accessories to turn the casual outfit up just a notch, I slid my feet into a pair of Coach sandals. I couldn't do an anklet today. My belly just wouldn't allow me to step up to that challenge.

I hit my body with a few generous sprays of Prada Paradox, grabbed my Coach bag to match my sandals, and headed out the door. Having been home the last few days, my car had been parked in the garage. Hopping inside my midnight blue Audi Q5, I put on my no skips R&B playlist that would take me through my hour ride into the city from my house in Jersey. Moving out of my apartment in Harlem into my house was the best thing I could've done. Having only my name on the house was the smartest.

My father was adamant that I didn't put Jalen's name on the house or a bill. His words were, *If that nigga wanna put his name on something, tell him to change yours first.* Needless to say, when it was time to sign on the dotted line, the only signature there was Amariyah Baker. Don't get it twisted though. Jalen still put money in my account to handle things, but when it came down to it, this was mine.

Pushing my seat back just a little to give my belly the space it needed, I turned on the AC and reversed out of the garage. Between the mini concert and little to no traffic on the highway, I made it to Harlem quicker than my usual time. Stepping out of the car, belly first, I put my shades on to protect my eyes from the sun. Entering the supermarket, I grabbed a Lysol wipe from my purse to wipe the handle of one of the shopping carts. People were trifling these days, so I made sure to have an all-purpose kit in my bag for times when I was out and about.

I already had the few things I thought Grandma would need in mind – eggs, bread, milk, cheese, paper towels, fruit, and a Pepsi. I could forget everything else, but that Pepsi was non-negotiable. The supermarket was my favorite place. From Fine Fare to Trader Joes, I loved walking up and down the aisles, checking for sales and completely disregarding the list I'd sorted by importance prior to arriving. I'd seen my mother and my grandmother do the same thing growing up, and they'd passed it down to me. I went to reach for the oat milk when my phone rang in my purse. Fishing it out with one hand, I grabbed the milk with the other.

Seeing my cousin, Tamia's name on the screen, I smiled before answering the FaceTime call.

"Good morning, Belly," she greeted with a bright smile.

"Hey, boo. What you up to? You look cute."

Stepping back, she did a full 360, her big curls bouncing all over her head and her sundress flowing in the air. **"You know I do my thang. I'm headed out on a breakfast date. Where you at?"**

"Grocery store for Grandma." Pushing the cart to the next aisle, I picked up her honey wheat bread.

"You out there grocery shoppin' like you ain't carrying a whole person that's due soon is so crazy to me. And I know Grandma Nita did not ask you to do that, Ms. Busybody."

Smirking, I shook my head, knowing she was right. **"Walking is good for me and the baby, Mia. Refer to my physician if need be. Besides, you know Grandma. She won't even say anything if she did need something. So, I just pop up with what I think she needs."**

"You know they created Instacart for people in your condition, right? You need my login?"

"I got one, boo. And I'm good. I promise. Besides, I've been cooped up in the house the last couple days, sorting out life, while planning to give life. Oh, and I put Jalen out." I threw in the last part casually as if it wasn't a big deal.

"Hol' up. Rewind." Picking up her phone from wherever she had it propped up, she brought it directly to her face. **"Out? Like, if you don't want me then don't talk to me. Go ahead and free yourself out?"**

I snickered at her reciting Fantasia's lyrics. **"More like, I'm headed to the laundromat. Nivea kinda out."**

"Ohhh," she dragged. **"And how are we feeling?"**

"Honestly, I feel relief. We weren't us anymore, and quite

frankly, I was tired of moving on empty threats. I'm not bringing my baby into any confusion. Jalen needed a wake-up call, and he got it today."

"That's what it is then, boo. As long as you're good with your decision, that is all that matters. Any updates on Happy Feet?"

Happy Feet was my baby's official nickname and for obvious reasons. The little girl just loved to tap dance in my belly.

"I seen my doctor last week. She said our girl is facing down in the birth canal, and we're all set for the water birth, at the birthing center."

"Perfect. I'm sure Jalen will be in attendance, but you call me if he decides to be a dickhead and not show up."

"I will." I smiled knowingly. Tamia would take on the world behind me with no questions asked.

"Alright. Let me go before I find a reason to change and be late to my date. I love you, boo. Send me a text when you make it to Grandma's."

"I love you too. And will do. Have a good time."

Ending the call, I picked up the last of my items and headed for the checkout line. I watched the cashiers at the registers, quickly assessing who would get me out the store faster by their scanning precision and speed. Deciding on the young cashier whose face looked like she'd rather be anywhere else but here, I pushed my cart in the direction of her register. There was a woman ahead of me who the cashier hadn't made eye contact with as she scanned her items. By the exchange, the woman seemed irritated.

"Oh, uhn uhn. There's a sign over there that says these Frosted Flakes are $2.99. They just scanned for $5.99. You need to fix that shit," the woman pointed out in a tone I felt was unnecessary, but I kept my opinion to myself.

The young girl looked up, and upon closer inspection, I could tell she'd been crying and was on the verge of new tears.

She took a deep breath before replying. "The $2.99 deal is for the large size box, ma'am. You have the giant size."

Once the lady put her hand on her hip, I knew she was about to cut up. Judging by the leggings, oversized tee that was stretched at the neck, and black Uptowns that appeared too small from the way she stood, I knew she was a menace to someone somewhere. "First off, little girl, I know what the fuck I picked up," she spat. "This box was under the $2.99 sign. So, you may want to check your little circular."

"That won't be necessary," the cashier retorted. "I'm aware of the sale items, and this box isn't a sale item this week. Would you like for me to remove it from your purchase or continue scanning?"

"Bi…" the woman started, and I had to step in because she was doing the most.

"Excuse me," I interjected politely, "you're holding up the line, love, and I have somewhere to be."

She cut her eyes at me and then turned back to the cashier. "Take it off. I'll get it at another store. Clearly y'all on some bull-shit here."

The cashier set the box to the side and continued on with her job. Once the woman's items were bagged, she snatched them up and went about her way.

"Thank you," she said as she checked me out.

"No problem." I swiped my card, while she walked around to put the bags in my cart. "Thanks, love."

Handing me my receipt, she nodded. "Have a good day."

"You have a better one. And keep your head up. You can't make the situation better if you're looking down, boo. You got this." I didn't know what she was going through, but I hoped my words were the encouragement she needed in the moment.

By the time I got to Grandma Nita's, baby Amari reminded me of just how pregnant I was. The heaviness I felt in my lower belly had me moving slow as I eased out of the front seat and into the back to grab the two grocery bags. With my purse secure on my shoulder, I locked the car and proceeded to walk across the street. The scene was the same as it had always been on a hot day in New York. The streets were littered with people. Kids ran up and down the block unsupervised, the seniors sat on their posts outside the building, while the hustlers manned the corners.

As usual, everyone seemed preoccupied with their own thing for the most part. It was home to my grandmother, and no matter how much we offered to take her out the hood, it was where her heart was. Everyone on the block knew GNani, and nobody fucked with her. And it wasn't just on the strength of my father's name either. She had her own rep that preceded her.

Greeting the seniors with a smile, I entered the building. My smile quickly dropped when I saw the sign taped to the elevator doors that read OUT OF ORDER. What were the odds that both elevators would be out when it was my day to visit? I instantly caught an attitude thinking about the three flights I'd have to walk up to get to the apartment. Glancing down at the bags in my hand, I sighed, walking over to the side door where the steps were.

I took instant offense as I stared up at the eight steps before me and the two additional flights that awaited me. "Ughhh, this is some bullshit," I grumbled with each step I climbed.

Getting up the first flight was work, but that goddamn second flight was a challenge I wasn't ready for. Setting the bags down on the floor, I held my back with one hand and cradled my belly with the other. Taking a deep breath, I had to coach myself to keep moving. As I approached the third-floor landing, I could hear moaning followed by a man's voice.

"Yeah, eat that dick up. Just like that. Gimme dat throat, shorty."

Disgusted, I turned the corner and was able to place the guy's face immediately. Jamel.

"Oh, shit," he said, jumping a little and pulling his dick from the girl's mouth.

Although irritated by their bold move, I couldn't help but notice the length and girth of his hard piece that was still wet from her saliva. *And a nice piece it was,* I thought. I secretly salivated while outwardly shaking my head with a look of disappointment.

"Y'all do know that this is a whole stairwell, right? And the elevators out, so people **have** to take the steps."

"There's two," the girl said, standing and wiping the corners of her mouth. She had no shame, and by her response, I could tell it wasn't her first stairwell visit.

"Yeah, well, I'm sure nobody wants to walk into either and see a woman on her knees," I fired back.

"My bad." Jamel offered an apology with a sheepish grin while adjusting his shorts.

Glancing down at my bags then back up to both of them, I shook my head.

"I'ma catch up witchu, Brandy," he said to the girl whose face twisted up at the thought of being dismissed.

"Catch up with me?" she repeated, her attitude heavy.

Shit, mine would have been too if I was caught with a dick in my mouth, and now the man attached to that dick was getting rid of me.

"Yeah."

"What the fuck ever, Melly!" she snapped before stomping past me down the steps.

"I guess you caught me slippin', huh? You need help with the bags?"

Jamel, affectionately known as Melly to the block, was a fine specimen. He towered over my 5'7" frame, at least an even 6'3", and had brown skin with a smile that still lingered in your head after you looked away. He had a swag about him that couldn't be denied. His long dreads were pulled to the back of his head in a low ponytail, exposing the tattoos on his neck and chest. I was a sucker for a tattooed man. And Melly was tatted down to his legs, which were firm like he was committed to the gym.

We'd only said a few words to each other in passing over the years, usually when I was coming to see my grandmother or leaving out. He was always polite. Always openly flirting with me but never to the point where it got overbearing. It was smooth, like he was testing the waters.

Admittedly, I liked it. The compliments he threw my way made me blush along with the promises of having me one day. I made sure to remind him that it would be in his dreams only. I was taken at the time, and to add to that, I was thirty-two, which made me six years older than him. A YN could do nothing with me.

"Caught you slippin' bad. Y'all bold and real nasty to be doing that in the staircase though. You betta be glad my grand-mother ain't see you." I chuckled and started past him up the steps again.

He laughed. "She would've cussed me and ol' girl out. You sure you don't need any help? You're already carrying a heavy load." He gestured toward my belly.

"We good. I carried us this far."

"Aight. Take it easy. You look like you bout to walk her right up outta there."

Stopping at the top step, I looked back with a raised brow. "How you know what I'm having?"

"GNani told me. I got you something. Dropped it off to her yesterday."

"Why?" I questioned.

He chuckled and shrugged. "It's the kinda nigga I am,

Amariyah. I'll see you around, shorty." I watched as he jogged down the steps until he disappeared from my sight.

His smooth, young ass, I thought as I pushed through the door into the hallway.

I didn't get to turn my key to unlock the door before it was done for me, and my grandmother pulled it open. "Come on in here so I can cuss you out for being hardheaded. Just like yo daddy." She grabbed the bags from my hands as I walked through the door.

"Why you gon' cuss me out? What I do?"

"Tamia called and said you was out at the grocery store shopping for me. When I ask you to do that, Mari?" Setting the bags in the kitchen, she put her hands on her hips and cocked her head to the side.

The small woman dressed in a satin muumuu with matching head wrap and slippers was as feisty as they came. To be only 5'4", my grandmother had the presence of a giant. She wasn't one of those older women who walked around hunched over either. She may not have been able to get around as fast, but let her tell it, she was still living out her younger years.

"I just got you a few things to restock. She acting like I went food shopping. Dang, I left your paper towels in the backseat."

"Good. Take 'em to your house because I'm fully stocked. Hey, GNani's baby." She rubbed my belly and gave it a kiss. "Ya mama out here doing the most. Ooouu, I should kick yo ass too. Ain't the elevators out?"

"Yeah. That's what took me so long to get up here." Grabbing my back, I winced a little.

"Girl, come in here and sit down." She guided me to the living room and helped me sit on the couch. "Didn't none of them niggas outside offer to help you with the bags?"

"Jamel did after I caught him in the hallway getting his thing sucked."

"His what?" She laughed.

"His thing." I smirked.

"Girl, that is a young man, say dick. And you should've let him help you still. He is a sweetheart. The only young one I like around here. Got a good heart. He come from good people."

"Mmmhmm. Ooouu, I gotta pee." Using the arm of the couch, I pushed myself up.

"Well, here, let me help you."

"I got it, Grandma. I'm good," I assured her.

"Now you see how I feel when y'all do that shit to me."

"Ahhh, you love it," I teased, turning the corner and walking down the hall to the bathroom.

As I got up to wipe myself, a sharp pain shot across my stomach, catching me off guard. Grabbing the sink, I sucked in air and gritted my teeth. Breathing through it, I wiped myself and pulled my shorts back up. Leaning over the sink, another pain hit, this time stronger than the first.

"Grandma!" I yelled out.

"What? What's wrong?" I heard her call back to me before I could hear her slippers heading my way. "Is the door unlocked?"

"Yes," I replied, now holding onto the sink with both hands, in pain.

"You in pain?"

I nodded, rocking from side to side and doing my best to breathe through what I knew were contractions. "I… I think I'm in labor," I whispered, placing my hand on my belly.

"Well, we ain't bout to stick around here and find out. Let me go throw something on. Come on, let's get you to the couch first."

"Wait, Grandma. Ouchhhh!" I yelped as another contraction hit me with force. "I can go. Let me call… Oouuu, shit. This shit hurts." The contractions were making it known that if it wasn't labor, something was going on.

"We can call them on the way." As she guided me back to the living room, there was a knock on the door. "Now, who the hell is this?" she asked, gently sitting me down and going over to it. "Who is it?"

"It's Jamel, G."

"Oh, good." Snatching the door open, she pulled him inside.

"Hey, G. I was just comin' to…"

"She's in labor." She pointed to me. "I need you to take her to the hospital."

"What?"

"Huh?"

"Y'all both sound dumb," she retorted. "The hospital. She needs to go. I need you to take her and stay with her. Come on." She pulled him by his shirt over to me. Noticing my hesitance, she wagged her finger at me. "It's not up for debate, Amariyah."

Blinking up at Melly, I gritted my teeth through another contraction. "You don…"

"Come on, shorty. I got you." As he helped me up from the couch, Grandma handed him my bag.

"Text me when y'all get there so I know where to come," she said to our backs.

"Aight, G," Melly responded like this was normal. "I know this shit weird, but I got you." Looking down at me, he smirked. "Let's go have a baby."

2

———

MELLY

$\mathcal{G}$etting caught with my dick out wasn't on the agenda for today, but shit, I'd been caught doing hella shit in the stairwell. Getting my dick sucked wasn't the wildest. Brandy had been on a nigga top for weeks, tryna see wassup, and I had been successfully dodging her advances. I didn't like a woman that came on too strong. But today, the way she was sucking on that Firecracker popsicle, I thought a lil' staircase action wouldn't hurt nobody.

And of all people to catch me slippin', it was Amariyah. I pulled my dick out of Brandy's mouth so fast, you would've thought she bit my shit. Although Amariyah didn't say more than a few words, it was the look that she gave me. It was a look of disappointment mixed with intrigue, like she expected more from me but also didn't expect a young nigga like me to be carrying around all this dick.

However, the part that stuck out was the initial disappointment. Not Brandy stomping off. Not the moment itself. But her reaction. Thing was, I didn't know why it hit me like that. Amariyah and I didn't have a past. We were cordial.

Our families knew each other, so I knew she came from

good people. I loved to see her smile, and every time we did come in contact with each other, I hit her with a compliment. There was something unspoken between us. Something I felt we both knew but neither one of us took a step to explore. She had a quiet confidence about her, like she wasn't pressed about anything or anyone. I liked that shit.

I made it downstairs to the lobby, hoping that I didn't run into Brandy. It was just my luck that when I swung open the doors to the stairwell, she was posted up against the mailboxes with her dick eating ass cousin, Taliah. Her back was turned to me, but one head nod in my direction from Taliah made her turn around. I didn't like that horse-mouth ass ho at all.

"Wassup, Melly?" Taliah spoke, and I ignored her as I often did. Snickering, she turned to Brandy. "I'ma run to the store right quick. I'll be back."

"Alright," Brandy replied before stepping toward me with her arms folded and lips poked out. "So, that's what it is? You gon' embarrass me in front of the next bitch?"

"Man, go head with that," I said, walking around her.

"Nah, ain't no go head with that," she countered, stepping in front of me. "You really just gon' play me like I ain't just..."

I took a step back and ran my hand down my face. "Be sure that you really wanna do this in the lobby cause you know once I blow, ain't gon' be nobody to save you." Public displays weren't my thing at all. I knew how I could get, and I wasn't gonna be the one left with the stuck face at the end of the day.

Shifting her weight to one side, she rolled her neck like she was ready for whatever. "I'm damn sure. You actin' like a bitch was beggin' you or somethin'. Like I didn't just do..."

"A mediocre job at best." I cut her off, and her mouth dropped.

"You know what? You a goofy ass nigga. Always walking around like you God's gift to a woman. You just like these other niggas, Melly. Yeah, you may have a name and be fine wit some money, but there's niggas finer with bigger bags."

Brandy wanted a reaction out of me, and unfortunately for her, I wasn't too in touch with my emotions, especially with someone who didn't mean shit to me.

I stared at her blankly and scratched my head. "How you feel now?"

"What?"

"To know you sucked a goofy nigga dick in the stairwell only to walk away wit a wet pussy and an attitude. How you feel?"

"Fuck you, Melly!" She stomped off for the second time, and I shook my head, laughing.

It fucked with Brandy's ego that as bad as she was, a nigga really ain't have no kick it for her. Shrugging, I tapped my pockets, remembering the other reason I'd come to the block today besides watering my aunt's plants while she was away – GNani's lotto tickets. She had me play the same numbers for her twice a week, Monday and Friday. According to her, the numbers were special, something about them coming to her in a dream from her late husband. I never questioned it, just played the numbers every week without fail.

Taking the steps back up to the third floor, I got to her apartment and knocked hard twice – twice only cause she didn't play that beating down her door shit. When she swung the door open, I didn't expect to be pulled inside by my shirt to see Amariyah rocking back-and-forth on the couch, holding her stomach.

"Come on, shorty. I got you," I said to her after GNani insisted I be the one to escort her to the hospital.

She was hesitant, and I understood why, but who was about to tell her grandmother no? It damn sure wasn't about to be me. As I helped her up from the couch, I slid an arm under hers, and she leaned into me. Even like this – sweating, breathing hard – she was still fine as hell. Her skin had a glow that had only been enhanced during pregnancy. I couldn't fully describe her face. All I could say was that she had delicate features, like she was made to be handled with care. Yet she had a presence that let you know that she could take care of herself.

Assuring GNani that we'd text her once we made it to the hospital, we made our way out the door.

"I know this shit weird, but I got you." I smirked. "Let's go have a baby."

"You say it like this is our child," she commented through calculated breaths.

Smirking, I continued toward the stairwell. As I went to push the door open, Mr. Calvin, the building's maintenance man, came out of the unit across from the stairs.

"The elevator's working," he informed, locking the apartment he'd just come out of.

"Why they got a sign on 'em that say they don't then?" I questioned while about facing and carefully guiding Amariyah over to the elevators.

Mr. Calvin shook his head and threw his hand up in annoyance. "Bad ass kids playing with the signs. Taping 'em back up after we took 'em down. Elevator been working."

"Y'all need to put something on the bulletin board then, Mr. C. People be having emergencies and shit." The elevator dinged, and the doors opened.

"I'm working on it, Melly."

"Ahhhh! Shit!" Amariyah froze as we stepped on and squeezed my shoulder, burying her face into my arm. "I'm sorry. I'm sorry," she said, not loosening her grip.

"You good, shorty. Ay, hit lobby for me, Mr. C."

He pressed the lobby button and jumped back just as the elevator doors closed.

"Here, let me hold your bag." I reached for her purse, and she handed it over without hesitation.

"You're gonna look so crazy walking out of here with my purse in your hand." She giggled lightly, her face still in my arm.

"And dare a nigga to say somethin' bout it. You sure you okay?" I asked as the elevator moved.

"I'm anxious and in pain," she admitted. "I'm thuggin' it out tho. I got this."

I nodded. "Yeah, you do. And I got you."

She glanced up at me with the same curious look she had earlier when she saw me in the stairwell – only softer. "You always this calm in crazy situations? Cause this is crazy."

"I'm calm when I need to be, Ma. You the one with the contractions. Somebody gotta hold it down."

"Ooouuu," she groaned, squeezing me again. Leaning forward slightly, she fought through.

I took the liberty of rubbing her back, slow and steady. "I'ma get you to the hospital as fast as I can."

"I need to get to the birthing center. I'm scheduled to have a natural birth. No hospital, no needles. Just me, the water, and peace. But here I am, sweatin' in an elevator. On my way to the hospital to be hooked up to a machine, surrounded by strangers. This wasn't my plan."

A tear fell down her cheek, and my chest tightened. Something about her expressing the heavy emotion had me ready to move heaven and earth to make sure she was able to have the birth she planned. The elevators dinged again and opened to the lobby where I moved as swift as I could to get her to my car.

"Ay, Melly, can I..."

I stopped James, the neighborhood beggar, in his tracks with a look before he could get close to me. "I'll holla at you later, Jay."

"I was just..." He tried to continue.

"What the fuck I just say?!" I roared, making Amariyah jump a little as I went to help her into the passenger side. "My bad," I said, easing her inside. Closing the door, I turned to James.

"Whatever you was about to ask, the answer is now no. All because you can't take a hint at your big ass age." Walking over to the driver's side, I opened the door.

"Wait," Amariyah said with her hand up. "There's a bag in my trunk. It's my hospital bag. Can you grab it for me? I can pop the trunk from here. I'm in the A…"

"Audi Q5," I finished her sentence. "Pop the trunk."

Jogging across the street, I opened the trunk and pulled out the only bag inside, a custom YSL duffle with the words, *Property of Amari's Mommy*. I smirked, thinking it was some fly shit. The beeping of my horn made me turn around. Amariyah was leaned over the center console, leaning on the horn and waving me forward. Closing her trunk, I went back over to my car, tossing her bag inside and jumping in the driver's seat.

"We gotta go. I feel a lot of pressure down there, and the contractions are coming more frequent."

"Okay. What's the address to the birthing center? You had a plan. Don't deviate from it."

"I can't…" she whispered.

"You can, and you **will**."

She sighed, and I grabbed her hand. "Gimme the address and let's make it happen. I'll call whoever you need me to call when we get there."

She rattled off the address, and I started up the car, pulling out of the parking spot with ease. Sneaking peeks over at her as I drove, I could see her typing on her phone with one hand and rubbing circles over her belly with the other. I smiled, turning my eyes back to the road just as her phone rang.

"**Hello,**" she answered softly. "**Yes, Toni. They're about three minutes apart now. Oouuu, hold on. There's one…**"

I volunteered my free hand, and she squeezed it. I didn't know where that manly strength came from, but she was holding on tight.

"**Okay, okay,**" she breathed, "**it passed. Hold on.**" She pulled the phone from her ear and held it in her hand. "**Can you hear me?**"

"**Yes,**" a woman said on the other end. "**How far are you from the birthing center, love?**"

"**About forty-five minutes.**"

"**Okay. I know you're gonna hate this, but with your contractions being three minutes apart, I'm sure it won't be long before they're closer. I need you to go to the nearest hospital. I can meet you there. I'd rather be safe than sorry, Amariyah. You and Mari's safety is first.**"

"**I understand,**" she said in a low voice filled with disappointment. "**Lenox Hill is close.**"

"**Okay. I'll meet you there. I'm not far. When you arrive, let them know you have a doula.**"

"**Alright.**"

"**Amariyah, you got this. It's a change of plans, but you're gonna be just fine.**"

"**Thanks, Toni. I'll see you in a minute.**" Ending the call, she dropped her phone back in her bag. Glancing down at her belly, she sang to it. "You are my world. My favorite girl."

The gesture was beautiful and soothing. She could carry a tune too.

"Hey," I called for her attention, and she looked up at me. "Peace ain't always a place, Ma. Sometimes, it's the person you're with. And sometimes, it's you knowing that you did something powerful on your own. Even if it doesn't go exactly how you planned."

Taking a deep breath, she nodded. Then, her face twisted. Instead of grabbing my hand this time, she hit the center console and twisted in her seat. As another contraction passed, she did that breathing shit you saw in the movies.

"I'm sorry."

"You good. I promise. We'll be to Lenox in ten minutes."

"You have kids?" she asked suddenly.

I glanced at her then back at the road. "Yeah. She up there chilling with God tho. Lost her during birth. Apparently, he needed her more than I did.

Her expression shifted, flashing empathetic eyes. "What is your angel baby's name? If you don't mind me asking."

"Cimani."

"That's pretty."

"Thanks, Ma."

"You think about having more?"

"Yeah. I fuck wit kids. The good ones." I smirked. "I'll terrorize the fuck out of a bad one. Five and up, I'm on they ass."

She laughed. "Melly, please. Five is…" she paused, grabbing my arm.

"Another contraction?"

Squeezing her eyes shut tightly, she nodded.

"Breathe. You got this shit," I encouraged, pulling onto E. 77th Street where Lenox Hill Hospital was located.

"I'm scared," she admitted then retracted her statement. "Well, not scared. Nervous. I'm nervous. I didn't expect it to be like this."

"I'm sure no mother does. Anybody you want me to call for you? I gotta text G." Parking my car, I got out to grab her bag from the back before going around to the passenger side door to get her.

"I texted my cousin. She should be here soon."

I wanted to ask about the father, but I wasn't the type of nigga to ask questions when I didn't care to know the answer, so I left that alone. As we walked through the doors of the ER, she squeezed my hand tight, stopping short.

"Contraction?"

She shook her head. "My water just broke."

Averting my eyes to the ground, I could see a small puddle.

"Oh, shit. Ay, I need help right now! Her water just broke!" My voice boomed.

The lady at the front desk snapped into action quick, grabbing a wheelchair and helping Amariyah into it. "Is she your wife?" the woman questioned.

I looked her dead in the eye and didn't hesitate before answering. "I'm the father."

Amariyah's head whipped in my direction, surprise written all over her face, but she said nothing. Slinging the duffle bag over my back, I placed both of my hands on the back of the wheelchair.

"Where we go?" I asked the woman who gave a half smirk like she knew I was up to bullshit but didn't call me out on it.

"I'll escort you two up to Labor and Delivery."

In the moment, I wasn't sure what this was or what it would become. I just knew that I'd given G my word. And I wasn't leaving her side.

3

AMARIYAH

I didn't know if someone had gotten the memo about my birthing plan or what, but things were going surprisingly smooth as I prepared to deliver my baby girl. The lights in the hospital room were soft, and the nurses assigned to me weren't rushing or moving carelessly. Everyone was in sync and polite in the way they were handling me. It was nothing like the chaotic environment I'd envisioned. I was thankful for that.

The OB on call, a Black woman with fresh boho knotless braids pulled up in a bun, introduced herself as Dr. James. When she walked in, it was as if she'd brought a light air with her. Her voice was soothing, and the way she took the time to walk me through everything while pausing and lending her hand to me through my contractions made me calm. Her energy made me feel like I had my homegirl in the delivery room with me until Tamia and my doula, who I'd taken a liking to, arrived.

"We're going to do our best to support your birth plan, Amariyah," she said while snapping her gloves on. "This is you and baby's show." She tossed me a genuine smile, and I nodded with one of my own.

"Thank... you... so much," I managed to get out while

breathing my way through another contraction. I'd declined the epidural as soon as they put me in the room. I wanted to stick to the script for as long as I could.

The scent of lavender and jasmine filled the room, courtesy of the diffuser I'd brought in my duffle bag. I also brought my own gown to wear, that I had made through a connection of Toni's, along with matching fuzzy socks with the grippers at the bottom. Was it over the top? Most would think so, but for me, it was all about being comfortable and having control over what was in my control. I had no say so on when Amari would make her debut, but I could make sure I was cute, and at peace as I laid in wait for her arrival.

I was currently six centimeters dilated, and the way the contractions were coming, I knew I'd be at ten in no time. If my water breaking in the middle of the emergency room wasn't surprising enough, the fact that Melly hadn't left my side after claiming to be my child's father threw me for a loop. It didn't make it no better that her real father hadn't even bothered to answer his phone when I called. And one call and a text was all he was getting out of me. I was so shocked by Melly's claim; I couldn't find the words to refute it.

Still, I didn't expect him to stick around after letting Grandma know that I made it safely. Yet, he was seated in a chair in the corner like he belonged there. His eyes scanned everyone and everything in the room as if he were hired to monitor me and "his baby". He didn't speak much other than the occasional *"You good?"* and *"You got this"* whenever a contraction hit hard. Other than that, he remained silent. Quiet comfort. Although it was odd, I appreciated his presence.

As Dr. James prepared to check my cervix again, there was a soft knock at the door. One of the nurses went over to open it, and there was Toni. She breezed in with her locs wrapped up in a messy bun on her head, her signature hoop earrings and wrist full of gold bangles that jiggled with each step she took. She sported an oversized tee with a picture of Lauryn Hill on it and a pair of loose-fitting joggers. Toni looked more like she was going to hang out at her favorite cousin's house than coming to assist with delivery.

"Good morning, everyone," she sang. "We're ready to have a baby, huh?" She was normally chill, but today, she had a little extra pep in her step.

Her face had a glow to it and not just from good skin care. No, Toni had gotten some dick care prior to arriving. I knew a *I just got my back blown out* walk when I saw it. Making her way over to me with a smirk, she set her bag down.

"You good?" I asked with a smile.

Grinning, she slapped her hands together. "I'm great! Let's have us a baby!"

Giggling, I turned to Dr. James. "This is my doula, Toni, that I mentioned."

"Nice to meet you, Toni," Dr. James greeted. "I would shake your hand, but I'm about to…" She pointed between my legs.

"Oh, it's no problem." Leaning over, she gave me a half hug then gently rubbed my belly. "Are you centered?"

"Trying to be. The aroma therapy is working."

"Good, good. You got this, girl." She embraced me again, and this time, I was able to get a whiff of cologne lingering on her body.

I had a keen sense of smell, so although the cologne was mixed with whatever brand of vanilla body butter she had on, I knew the scent. **Dior Sauvage.** It was a scent I'd come to know well, one that I'd replenished countless times. It was Jalen's signature scent. Inhaling once more, I nodded in recognition but said nothing. There was nothing to say. My intuition never steered me wrong.

However, the fact that I was about to bring life into the world made it trivial to speak on at the moment. So, I filed it away until the time was right to bring it to the forefront.

"Let me wash my hands." Turning from me, I watched as she practically glided over to the available sink in the room.

Dr. James proceeded to check my cervix, making me squirm a little. "Alright, we're at eight centimeters. Almost there, Mommy. I'm going to step out for a few minutes, and I'll be right back." Pulling my gown down, she gave me a reassuring smile and headed out. The nurses followed behind her.

I could hear ringing coming from Toni's bag, and before I could call out to her, she beelined toward it.

"Well, damn," Melly let out, finally making his presence known. "They must be important as fuck."

Toni's head shot in his direction. I wanted to check him and laugh at the same time.

"Ummm, I gotta get this," she announced. "I'll be right back." With her phone clutched tightly in her hand, she gave Melly another look before exiting.

Sitting up in his chair, he whispered, "You sure you want shorty to coach you through this? I mean, I thought I was doing a pretty good job. And of the two of us, I'm the only one who don't look like I just came off a fucking spree."

My eyes widened, and he rushed to my side.

"What? Contraction? Pain?"

I couldn't help but laugh at the concern on his face. "Neither right now. I just can't believe you said that."

"Said what?" he asked with a genuine look of confusion.

"What you just said?"

"What? That your doula look like she been fucking before she got here?"

"Yes, crazy. Oh, wait, shhh." I grabbed the bed railing and breathed through a contraction. "Alright now, Happy Feet, you gon' have to come up outta there." Pushing myself up on the bed, I focused back on him.

"She ready to come up outta there."

"I know. I'm ready to see her. Back to what you said though.

Yes, I recognized the glow on Toni, but I hired her. She's good at this."

"Shit, me too. I mean, I was front and center when Cimani came out. I had to be."

"I appreciate that, but I think she's got it handled."

"Respect," he conceded. "Can I ask you a question?"

"Sure."

"Where yo nigga at?"

I smirked. "As of 9:52 this morning, I don't have one."

"Noted."

We stared at each other for a few seconds, only breaking eye contact when the door to my room swung open.

"Whoo, I made it just in time. I'm here, GNani." I heard Tamia's voice, and Melly moved to the side for me to see her. "Oh, bitch, not you in the bed wit yo own shit on." She laughed, walking over to me with her phone to her ear. **"Hold on, GNani. Here she go."**

"Hello?" I spoke into the phone. I caught my grandmother up on my progress, making sure to leave out the part about Jalen not showing up or answering his phone. Unfortunately, I had to tell Tamia. **"Yeah. He's still here. Acting like security."** I glanced up at Melly and held the phone out to him. "She wants to talk to you."

Taking the phone from me, he brushed his fingers across mine before stepping off to the side. **"Wassup, G?"** he said.

"His young ass is fine as hell. I can't get over how much he looks like Capella Grey."

I nodded, agreeing with her assessment. "I'm so happy you're here. And before you ask, I called Jalen. He didn't answer. End of story."

She shrugged. "Shit, that's his loss. He just pushed you right into the arms of the next nigga. A young one at that."

Another contraction hit, followed by the urge to push. "Get Toni and the doctor, Mia. I gotta push. I gotta push now."

Melly spun around, locking eyes with me, as Tamia rushed out to get my help.

"I ca…"

Seeing his look of concern, I spoke clearly. "It's okay. You can stay."

<hr>

THE LOVE THAT RADIATED OFF MY BODY FOR THE LITTLE HUMAN I now held in my arms was something I couldn't describe. After six intense pushes, she made her way through. Her cries filled the room, sharp, loud, and beautiful. Dr. James held her up, and tears slid down my face. She was mine.

Amari Story. Mommy's everything.

She lay in my arms, wide awake, staring up at me with her little fist balled up tight as if she knew the things that had gone through my head over the past twenty-four hours before her arrival.

"Actin' like her mommy already," Tamia commented, standing on the side of me. "She's perfect, cousin."

"I know, right?" I agreed, not taking my eyes off her.

Her chestnut brown skin tone mirrored mine, along with her little nose, eyes, and lips. I had undoubtedly birthed a miniature version of myself. Tracing a finger over her soft cheeks, I silently thanked God for getting us both through it. With the alarming rate of Black women dying during childbirth, I didn't take the moment for granted.

My eyes found Melly's just as he looked up from his phone and gave me a nod. While I was sure everyone had their thoughts about his presence, no one voiced them. And not that they would have had a right to, especially since his support didn't come from a place that felt like he was pushing himself on me. He was cool.

"Alright, boo, I have to go check on the shop. You good here?" Tamia questioned.

"Yep. I'm great."

Her eyes shifted toward Melly, who nodded at her. "I'm sure you are." She smirked. "You need anything before I go? I know hospital food be so trash, and you've been here a few hours."

I snickered, shaking my head. "No. I'm okay for now. If anything, I can order something on Door Dash."

"Okay, cool. I love you. I'll check in on you later." Leaning over, she kissed my check and the top of Amari's head that was now covered in a small hat with a bow that GNani knitted. She nodded at Melly as she left, and he responded with a smile. Tamia was a trip.

Toni returned to the room a few minutes later after leaving out to take a phone call. She wasn't as jovial as she was when she first walked in. Her face was a little flushed, and it seemed like she was rushing. Making her way to me, she mustered up a smile.

"You did so good. And this little one is so perfect." She leaned over to look at Amari. "You okay?"

"I am. Thank you."

"Of course. You know, I never got to ask you who's the guy? It's like he's been here but not here." She giggled, trying to play off the fact that she was being nosey.

"I'm sure you never asked because you knew it wasn't your place to." I replied with a straight face. "But since you're curious, he's a friend of the family."

"Ohhhh, okay. He don't talk or nothing, girl." She fake laughed.

I shrugged. "Not good with strangers, I guess."

"Yeah, I get it," she said with a tight smile. "Well, I have to get going. I have another client who's in active labor now. It's just… wild today."

"Yeah. I bet."

Grabbing her bag from the chair next to the bed, she pulled it over her head. "You mind if I take a picture of this cutie before I go?" She held her phone up, and I quickly shut her down.

"I do mind," I said, soft but clear. "Not ready to put her on display yet."

Pausing, she slowly put her phone away. "I completely understand. Whenever you get around to taking photos, I'd love to have one for the baby gallery at the birthing center."

"Okay. Thanks for your help."

"No problem. And congrats again, Amariyah." She dipped quickly.

Once the door closed behind her, Melly got up from his seat.

"You can breathe easy now, Ma. Shorty gone."

"What?" I questioned, adjusting Amari in my arms.

"I'm saying, you were relaxed until she came back in here. Then, you got all tense and shit."

"Now, how you see that from where you was sitting? And I was not tense."

"Mannnn, if looks could kill, Erykah Badu would've been DOA. Then you clutching the baby all tight. I was tryna make eye contact with you to see if you wanted me to get rid of her ass."

I laughed. "She asked who you were. Said you don't talk or nothing."

"Shiiiddd, she should be grateful I didn't talk. I be saying some off the wall shit sometimes. I would've definitely asked if she had just come from fucking when she got here."

"Something is wrong witchu." I smiled, shaking my head.

"She's beautiful," he complimented, looking down at Amari. "You handled that shit like a soldier, shorty. Real woman king type shit."

"And did." I replied proudly. We shared a laugh that was interrupted by my ringing phone. "Oouu, can you pass me that?" I asked, pointing to it on the end of the table.

"I got you." Grabbing the phone, he handed it to me.

I rolled my eyes seeing Jalen's name flash on the screen. I answered, even though everything in me said *fuck him.*

"**Hey,**" I said, my tone flatter than a Pepsi with the cap left half open.

"**You called?**" he asked, sounding dumb.

"**Do you have a missed call from me, Jalen?**"

"**Yeah.**"

"**Okay, so, let's not play this game,**" I retorted, my tone laced with irritation.

"**You good?**"

"**Just fine. Me and Amari.**" One cue, she whimpered.

"**You had her?**"

"**Yes. About an hour ago actually.**"

The phone went silent, and then, I heard shuffling. "**You okay? Is she okay? You did it alone?**"

Tilting my head up, my eyes found Melly's. Only his were on Amari's, making goofy faces. "**I was in good company,**" I replied confidently.

"**...You cool wit me pulling up?**"

I rolled my eyes in irritation. What father asked to come and visit their newborn? My first thought was to tell him to go to hell, but then I remembered my vow to **never,** under any circumstances, let my personal feelings about my child's father effect my child. So, with disdain, I agreed. I had some shit I needed to get off my chest regarding my suspicions anyway. After letting me know he'd be by shortly, I hung up before he could.

"That's my cue," Melly let out. "Unless you need me to stay? I don't know what the relationship is between you and yo bd, but it don't sound like you fuck wit him too tough."

"I can handle it. Thank you for doing this, Melly. You really didn't have to. I appreciate it."

"No thanks needed, Ma. Ay, can I ask you another question?"

"Shoot."

"This is no disrespect intended at all. How old are you?"

I giggled. "I'm thirty-one, nosey. Why?"

"Just asking. I know your people sliding through and shit but take my number in case you need anything."

"Okay." Unlocking my phone, I went to my contacts to add a new number. "Go head," I said, prompting him to read his number off to me.

"Lock me in under Melissa."

"What?" I frowned.

"Shit, ion know what you and yo bd got going on. And I ain't tryna get you caught up. That and I will definitely pop that nigga."

I found myself turned on by that gangsta shit. I had to keep a straight face, so he wouldn't know it. "You're going in here under Melly. I don't have nothing to hide. And if you got something to hide, don't save my number at all," I said matter-of-factly.

"Got you. If you need anything, *call me*. Enjoy your princess." He winked at me and proceeded to leave out.

His young ass had a swag on him that couldn't be ignored.

"Mommy gotta calm her hot pocket down, Mari. You almost had a step daddy just that quick." Kissing my little baby's head, I lifted myself from the bed and placed her in the bassinet.

I wanted to get a little sleep to prepare myself for Jalen's arrival. I had no plans on arguing nor doing the back-and-forth thing. I planned to ask questions, and I knew if he didn't provide verbal answers, his demeanor would tell it all.

<hr>

By the time Jalen walked into the hospital room, I had slept, taken a walk around the Labor and Delivery unit with Amari, and had a shower with the assistance of one of the nurses. I'd even changed into a lounge set to further my comfort. My ass was clean, hair was pinned up, and Amari was knocked out after some titty milk. Oh, I was prepared to let a nigga have it.

He stepped into the room slow, eyes scanning the area as if someone would jump out on him. Before he could even get close, I could smell him. **Sauvage**. His scent mirrored Toni's. Only on her, it was more subtle.

He looked good. His hair was freshly lined, crisp white tee, and a pair of ChromeHeart sweats hung off his waist. Real chill. Relaxed. Very *just was fuckin' earlier.*

"Hey," he spoke, heading for the bassinet where Amari lay, sleep.

"Hey," I replied.

"Look at her. She knocked out." He went to reach into the bassinet and paused, turning to me. "You got hand sanitizer? I know how you do." He laughed nervously.

"I prefer you use soap and water." I pointed to the sink, and he went over to it.

"How you feeling?" he asked, looking over at me as he washed his hands.

"Ready," I uttered with warning.

"To go home? I bet."

I didn't bother correcting him. Just let him move about and visit with his daughter.

"I don't wanna move her." He hovered over the bassinet, rubbing her head. "She got your whole face. Nah." He chuckled. "She got her fist balled up like she ready to start some shit." Stepping back for me to see, he had her blanket pulled back a little, showing her little fists.

"She's her mother's child for sure," I replied coldly.

Wrapping her back up, he turned to me fully. "Amariyah…"

I cut him off. "How long you been fucking Toni?"

He froze with the stuck face, making me want to launch my phone at him. "What?"

I scoffed, shaking my head. "You just told me what I needed to know by responding with a question as opposed to an answer."

He stood silent, staring at everything but me. For a brief moment, I was glad that he didn't try to further insult my intelligence by making up a lie on the fly.

"It wasn't…"

"No, Jalen," I silenced him with my hand, feeling myself levitate from the bed. "You didn't just cross a line. You hopscotched over that motherfucka. You couldn't pick someone that I didn't entrust with *my body* and *my birth*? Like damn. And what's crazy is you probably would've been able to pull the shit off too had she not come in here smelling like you." As I ranted, something dawned on me that pushed me off the bed. "Hol' on. Were you with this bitch when I called and texted that I was having contractions, nigga?"

He lowered his head, his silence saying yes before his mouth could even form the words.

"Damn," I whispered, taking a step back. "It's cool." I nodded. "It's so cool."

"Mari, that shit only happened a few times. I'm not gonna make any excuses cause I was dead wrong. I… I'm sorry."

The shame on his face didn't move me.

"After this, I'll never look at you as anything more than Amari's dad." My words were cold, clear, and final.

Jalen knew me well enough to know that there was no sense in saying anything else on the subject. Other than co-parenting, we were a dead issue.

4

MELLY

Being in the room with Amariyah while she gave birth really shifted something in a nigga. Although I was prepared to keep my word to GNani and not leave her side, I wasn't prepared for her to actually want me to stay. Still, I kept my distance, making sure I was seen and not heard unless she needed me. My silence wasn't just due to me wanting to remain low but also because being in the delivery room brought back memories that I still found myself trying to suppress. I felt that slow, heavy ache that used to sit on my chest everyday resurfacing.

The moment she pushed baby Amari out, my heart sank. While she didn't look anything like my little girl, who came out almost white, the headful of hair and tiny fingers gripping the air was familiar. Amari let out a wail that let the world know she was here. One that I never got a chance to hear. My daughter didn't get a chance to cry, breathe, or hold my finger.

Cimani was born a year ago. There had been no complications during the pregnancy. Shit was almost too perfect if you asked me. Her mother didn't swell up, didn't experience Braxton Hicks contractions, or none of that. There were no signs that anything was wrong when we did checkups either. Everything was going well in the delivery room... until it wasn't. Somewhere between the last push and the doctor trying to suction her out, her umbilical cord wrapped around her neck twice.

They called it asphyxia. Said my baby died from lack of oxygen due to the cord not being unwrapped in enough time. I said it was crazy as fuck how the same thing that transferred oxygen and nutrients to essentially assist in my baby's growth ended up killing her. Shit was crazy. And to hear the medical professionals constantly tell us, *"This is just a thing that happens sometimes,"* did absolutely nothing to ease our pain.

We were wrecked. Fucked me up so bad, I swung on the doctor, connecting right at that nigga's jaw. They put me out, but no charges were filed. Them people understood where it was coming from. They had to.

Paige hadn't been the same since. She didn't just blame the hospital. She blamed herself. She blamed me. And eventually, she blamed the world. Each day that passed, she got colder, sinking into a dark place that not even her friends and family could pull her out of. As her man, I remained on the frontline, stepping into that dark place with her. Mourning beside her.

Somehow, she didn't see it that way. She started lashing out. Letting me know I could never feel the pain she felt, no matter how much I thought I did. That shit was like a knife through my heart. Paige didn't understand that while she was in a dark place, a nigga was trying to keep from sinking myself. She didn't understand that me sinking would've had me in a cell facing life. My head was so fucked up, I had to stay away from niggas, knowing that any wrong move would set me off.

I tried to stay, but I couldn't breathe with her hatred hanging over me. There was no loving her through it because she didn't see the other side. Our daughter was gone, but we still had to live for her. Paige was choosing to suffer, but I could no longer suffer with her. So, I left.

It turned out to be the best thing for us. Lately, we'd been calling, texting, and even chillin' every now and then. It was nothing serious, and it was clear that we were both single. But the familiarity made it easy for us to be around each other… sometimes. She'd texted twice while I was at the hospital, but I didn't respond until the last one.

> Paige: You know… if you're having one of those
> days where you don't wanna be bothered, you
> can just say that, Melly. Ignoring me is crazy.

> Me: I was handling something. I'm headed your
> way now.

Leaving Amariyah with my number to call if she needed anything, I left before her bd arrived. Although part of me wanted to stay to keep her company, I ain't want the nigga to show up and get to acting stupid. I didn't know him or know of him, but my *back a nigga down* was universal, so it wouldn't have mattered. It didn't take nothing but a feeling for me to click out.

I pulled into the driveway of Paige's townhome forty-five minutes later and parked behind her Range Rover. Paige came from money. Her people weren't well off, but because of the many businesses in their family, they had some bread. One of those businesses was one of the most popular barbershops in the city that her uncle owned – a shop where I'd worked the last two years, becoming one of the most sought out barbers.

Up until recently.

I'd been working more outside the shop. Taking on more clientele and exploring other opportunities. Between cutting hair, going to school, and dibbling and dabbling in the weed market here and there, the money was coming in steady enough to where I didn't have to work around nobody's schedule but my own. The way I liked it.

Stepping out of my car, I checked my phone to see if Amariyah had called or texted. Seeing she hadn't, I slipped the phone back into my pocket. I didn't know why I thought she would've reached out. She'd just given birth. The baby was her focus, and I could already tell by the way she gazed into her daughter's eyes that she was the woman for the job of motherhood.

Making my way up to Paige's door, she pulled it open before I could knock. Dressed in a pair of little ass shorts, a sports bra, and curls over her head, she leaned against the door.

"Where you been?"

"Helpin' out a friend," I said, stepping past her and into the house. "Ended up being out longer than I expected. You cooked?"

"What *friend*? I ain't never known you to be the friendly type outside of your circle. You ain't gotta lie to soothe me, Melly. If you were out wit a bitch, you can say that."

"Sounds like you're mixing the question you really wanna ask with an assumption. And last I checked, we wasn't even on it like that. So, I'll opt out of responding to both. Did you cook?"

"No. I didn't cook. And I don't need a reminder of where we stand. You make that clear every time I try to have a serious conversation with you."

"I ain't come here to have a serious conversation, Paige. My noodles in the cabinet?" I asked, heading to the kitchen. Paige ate a lot of healthy shit that I didn't like. I made sure to keep a stash of shit I liked in my own designated cabinet.

"Yeah," she replied, following behind me. "The same five packs are still there. You know I don't dabble in the poor man's meal."

Ignoring her as she hopped up on the counter, I washed my hands. She wanted to be bougie so bad, but we both knew that if

I put the Top Ramen in a pot with some potatoes, her ass would have a fork out, ready to dig in.

"Is this *friend* the reason why you ain't been showing up at the shop to cut lately?"

Emptying the contents of the soup packet into a bowl, I poured water over it and popped it in the microwave. "I've been cuttin'. Just not at the shop."

She tilted her head with a judgmental look on her face. "So, you freelancin'?"

"Ay, Bronx12 News, fuck is up with the twenty-one questions?" I questioned, already annoyed, and I hadn't been in the house five minutes.

"I'm just saying why keep thinking small? You're one of the top barbers in a **prime** shop."

"I'm **thinking** about what works best for **me**," I replied. "Not you or anyone else. You already know I'm doing this school shit to get my business degree, so I can get my own spot. I can only go but so far building under somebody else's roof, Paige."

Her eyes narrowed, and she shook her head. "My uncle gave you that seat, Jamel. He saw your potential and gave you an opportunity. You just gon' walk away from it?"

"First off, your uncle didn't **give** me shit. And there wasn't any potential for him to see because a nigga name was ringin' for cutting prior to me meeting you and you introducing me to him. Yeah, being at his shop grew my clientele because of the name, and I appreciate that, but my skills is what got me in the door and what's gotten me this far. Don't get to talkin' like a nigga threw me a bone."

"I didn't mean it like that." Her voice softened a bit. She knew that she was about to piss me off and was trying to take another approach, but it wasn't working. Jumping down off the counter, she rubbed my arm. "I'm just saying you don't always have to get it out the mud. If there's an easier route to take, why not take it?"

"You mean let a nigga spoon feed me til' he feel like it's time for me to spread my wings? You know that ain't even me. No matter how bad you want it to be. Watch yo' head." I popped the microwave door open to grab my soup.

"So, you just gon' quit the shop?"

"Already did. Surprised your uncle didn't tell you that part since he so busy reporting everything else. My people gon' follow me wherever I go. Whether I'm cuttin' at his shop, in a trap, or in my own shit. I don't need to work for your uncle or anyone else to validate my skills."

She scoffed. "You're hardheaded as hell, you know that?"

"And you're entitled as fuck. Something we figured out a week into knowing each other." Stirring the seasoning into my noodles, I picked up my bowl. "We chillin' or we gon' keep talking about your dreams for me?"

"You wanna watch *Sinners*?" She got on board quick.

"Yeah. Then you can let me fuck that lil' attitude up out you." Smirking, I walked ahead of her and out to the living room. I knew I was a motherfucka to deal with and so did she. Yet, she was still here and not against her will.

It had been two days since I left Amariyah at the hospital. And while I'd been back to handling business, she'd crossed my mind a couple times. I still hadn't received a text or call, but I wasn't tripping. If anything, I just wanted to make sure she and the baby were alright.

"Sooo… you remember what you said last month, right?" I looked over at my little sister, Teeny, who was on the opposite side of the couch with a sly smile on her face.

We were lounging around my aunt's house after having picked her up from the airport. She'd been gone on vacation for two weeks, and Teeny had been staying with a cousin of ours.

Aunty Reece was our surrogate mother. Our biological mother, her younger, didn't want kids but insisted on having them to in some way appease my father and keep him around. That shit stopped working after she got pregnant with Teeny. He finally told her that he saw no future in the relationship and just wanted his kids.

I still couldn't understand why she reacted the way she did when he finally kept it real with her. They were together for thirty-two years on and off, and the man never put a ring on her finger. She walked around content with claiming to be his common law wife, and nigga baby mama off the strength of not wanting to start over. When he left, he kept in touch with us, making sure we had everything but his time. Shit, I would've much rather the nigga stayed because soon after, our mama became a figment of our imagination. If it wasn't for my sister, Tanisha, and my Aunt Reece, Teeny would've been lost.

I mean, I had her back as her big brother, but I couldn't teach her how to be a woman. It got to a point where my mother was cool on us and just dipped. It fucked Tanisha up, Teeny was too young to understand, and I had become so close to my Aunt Reece that my mother's presence really didn't matter to me. I had access to my father, but there was shit that he could do better, so I fucked with him from a distance. Over the years, Teeny was conjoined at my hip, looking to me for the guidance she refused to get from him. In her eyes, he was the reason our mother didn't want anything to do with us. I never tried to change her mind, just showed up like a big brother should.

"I say a lotta shit, Teeny. You gon' have to be more specific." I smiled back, already knowing what she was referring to.

She rolled her eyes and pouted. "Don't do that, Melly. You said that I could move in with you after graduation. Graduation is in two weeks, and now, you gotta stand on what you said."

Tilting my head, I pointed at my chest. "I said that?"

"Yes. You said that. And don't lie because T heard you too. I'll call her right now to confirm." She picked up her phone, and I laughed.

"You actin' like she gon' beat my ass or something. I remember what I said though, Teeny. You ain't gotta call no witnesses to the stand. You sure you wanna live with me? I don't keep no food in the crib, shit be messy, and I snore loud as hell. Sometimes, I wake my damn self up."

Grinning, she waved her hand in the air. "That's cap! You too greedy not to have food, and you hate mess. Now, that last part, I'ma have to agree with you on. It's only when you really tired though. Other than that, you straight."

I launched a decorative pillow at her that hit her in the head.

"Do I go to your house tossing your shit around, Jamel?" my aunt asked, walking into the living room.

"You don't even come to my house, Aunty."

"Boy, don't play with me," she said, slapping my arm and sitting on the couch next to me. "What y'all out here talking about?"

"This one tryna invade my space," I joked, pointing at Teeny.

"You have a three-bedroom apartment, Melly. You won't even know I'm there," Teeny advocated for herself.

"Oh, yes, the hell he will. Yo' presence is all over this house, girl." My aunt chuckled.

"You're not helping my case, Aunty."

"My bad," she said with her hands up.

"I'ma go call my sister, so we can talk about you." She pointed to me as she stood up from the couch and headed to her room.

"You sure you ready for that?" my aunt questioned.

I rubbed the back of my neck and stretched. "I already said I would. You know I'm not going back on my word."

"I know." She nodded, tapping my knee. "You just remember that she's not an adult yet. She's a seventeen-year-old young lady who still needs guidance. Structure. I know you like to be the friend."

"I got her, Aunty. She gon' be good."

"Yesss!" I heard Teeny say.

We both turned around just as she ducked her head back into the room.

"Ear hustling ass!" I laughed. My phone rang next to me on the couch with an incoming call from GNani. I answered on the second ring. **"Wassup, G. Everything okay?"** I asked, thinking about Amariyah.

"Yeah. Everything is good, baby. I was just reaching out to see if you mind swinging me by the hospital to see Mari and the baby. These Uber niggas tryna charge me forty dollars to go a few blocks. Now, I got it. I just ain't tryna give it to them."

"I hear you, G." I chuckled. **"I'm at my aunt's. If you ready now, I can meet you in the lobby in five minutes."**

"Okay. I'm leaving out the door now. I appreciate it. Tell your aunt I said hey and welcome back."

"Will do. I'll be downstairs." We ended the call, and I stood from the couch. "GNani said hey, Aunty."

"Tell her I said the same. Have you seen her granddaughter lately? I wonder if she had the baby yet."

"She did. Two days ago actually."

"Awww, okay. Tell her I said congrats. I know that baby too cute."

"Cute as fuck, Aunty. No cap." I concurred.

"How you know?"

"I was there when she gave birth."

"Oooo," she dragged, with a slow head nod. "I don't know how you pulled that off, nephew. But I see you." Grinning, she winked at me.

Leaving the house, I took the steps down to the lobby to get there faster. Pushing through the stairwell door, the elevator was just opening, and G stepped off it. She had on a Nike jogging suit with a fanny pack and a visor. GNani was dressed like she was going to get her steps in.

"You ready?" she asked.

"Yep."

Walking toward the exit, I held the door open for her. As we made our way down the ramp, Brandy and Taliah were coming up. Brandy rolled her eyes, and Taliah did the same with her cheerleading ass.

"I hope they rolling they eyes at you," G said, loud enough for the two to hear.

Neither said anything in response. They knew GNani was a better cusser than Yuntie Tia and would get on your ass in a heartbeat.

"They are," I admitted once we got to my car.

"Must've been one of them that you were in the staircase with the other day," she said, getting in on the passenger side.

Laughing, I didn't reply as I closed her door. This lady was a trip.

———

At the hospital, we were checked in as visitors and made our way upstairs to the maternity floor. When we reached Amariyah's hospital room, she was fully dressed, packing her bag.

"Girl," GNani called out, making her jump and spin around with her hand on her chest. "You ain't say nothing about being discharged today."

"Grandma, you scared the hell out of me. Hey, Melly." She waved. "What y'all doing here?" She embraced GNani.

"Well, I came here to see you and my gran, but you look like you're on the way out the door." GNani walked over to the bassinet to Amari, and I stayed planted near the door. "I had

Jamel bring me down. Where you going without no car and no car seat for the baby? And why you ain't call nobody?"

She asked the questions that were burning in my head.

Amariyah grimaced. "It was last minute. The doctor cleared us to go. I ordered her a car seat off Instacart that should be delivered any minute now, and I was gonna take an Uber to my car."

"An Uber?" GNani shook her head. "With your newborn, Amariyah? Ain't no way you have a baby and get dumb. You should've called me!"

"Or me," I chimed in.

Amariyah shot me a look that said I wasn't helping, and I shrugged.

"I didn't want to bother anybody. I'm up and moving. I had it, Grandma."

"I'm not even talking to you no more," GNani said, focusing on baby Amari. "When the car seat gets here, Melly will help put it together, and we'll get in his car to go home."

"Grandma, that's really not necessary. And you keep volunteering his services without asking is crazy. Making me sound like a charity case." Her frustration was evident, so I stepped in on my own behalf.

"You good, Ma. I did tell you to call me if you needed anything. If I didn't wanna be bothered, trust me, I don't have a problem letting you know. If it makes you feel any better, I can drive y'all back to G's crib, and you can get your car. Cool?"

She nodded. "You sure?"

"Positive."

"Alright. Thank you. I promise this is the last thing you'll have to do for me."

A nigga wouldn't mind doing things for you or to you, I thought to myself, licking my lips, but didn't speak. Just nodded. If Amariyah only knew.

5

———

AMARIYAH

*L*eave it to me to think I could escape the hospital without being caught by someone. I'd just hung up with GNani earlier in the day. She didn't mention anything about coming down to the hospital. But here she was, popping up. The way she called me out in front of Melly didn't upset me. My grandmother was feisty like that. And with the plan I just ran down to her, I didn't expect anything different. I didn't need him cosigning though.

After saying her peace, she focused on her gran, checking for all ten fingers and toes, noting how much she looked like my mother in the face. The comment made me sad. I missed my girl like hell. Bringing a baby into the world without either of my parents here to witness it was a reality I never saw coming. I couldn't wait for my father to call, so I could share the good news.

"Gotta make sure it's snug but not too tight for you in there, Lil Mama." Melly's baby talk pulled me from my thoughts as I watched him buckle Amari into what would now be her third car seat.

The way he took his time unboxing the car seat and ensuring

it was set up correctly made me feel warm inside. A thoughtful man. A man who showed up even when he didn't have to. I didn't know who needed reminding that Amari wasn't his – him or me. With focused brows, he adjusted the base and tested the straps twice.

"You straight, Mama?" he asked a two-day old Amari. "You gotta smile if you straight."

When she smiled, I threw my hand up to my mouth in shock. GNani laughed.

"Them post COVID babies something else, huh?" she said. "And you good at that, boy. Talkin' like you got some experience."

He smiled, stepping back for us to see his work. "I used to practice how I'd hold Cimani's car seat without losing my swag. Had to still be that nigga and a dad at the same time. You know, balance."

The room got quiet with the exception of the audible baby sounds coming from Amari. He glanced over at us, grinning, while GNani and I shared sad eyes.

"I think she's ready to go," he announced.

I cleared my throat and grabbed my bag. "Yes. I'm ready to get home," I said.

"You need a wheelchair, Mari?" GNani asked.

"No. I can manage on my feet. You mind carrying the car seat for me, Melly?"

"I got you," he replied, taking my duffle bag from me too. "And I'll take this."

We left the hospital looking like every bit of a family – Mom, Dad, Grandma, and baby. I was awkwardly comfortable, if that even made sense. Outside, the heat was thick compared to the well-ventilated hospital room.

Melly opened the passenger door for GNani then the back passenger door for me. I slid in first, and he placed Amari inside, securing the car seat in the seatbelt and the duffle bag next to it.

"Thank you," I said.

"You welcome, Ma."

Getting in the driver's seat, he pulled off and got on the freeway. As we drove, my phone vibrated in my purse. Reaching for it, a wide smile spread across my face. The caller ID read unknown. But the person on the other end was anything but that.

I answered on speaker and let the automated system do its thing before I greeted my heart.

"Hey, Daddy."

"Wassup, Daddy Princess. What you up to?"

"Ohhh, nothing. Just left the hospital with Happy Feet." I grinned.

"Whattttt?" he dragged, making me giggle. **"PJ here?"** he asked with a smile in his voice.

"Yes. Princess Jr. is here. And she's perfect just like you said she would be, Daddy." I peeked through the car seat cover, and Amari was asleep.

"Ahhh, man. I just know she is. Congratulations, Princess. When'd you have her?"

"Two days ago," I mumbled.

"Two days ago?!" he repeated. His tone elevated with more passion than anger.

"Hey," GNani let out from the front seat. **"Yell at your own grandbaby, not mine. As a matter of fact, don't yell at her either."**

"My bad, Mama. Y'all know I hate being the last to know shit. This ain't no regular news."

"Well, son, you know what your instructions were."

My father had his own personal phone that he usually called us on and only used the wall phone in the event of an emergency or if he had to switch phones. He was clear on his instructions when it came to the cell phone. We were not to call him; he would call us. With him calling from the state phone, I figured there was news he had to share.

"You right. I apologize, Princess."

"It's okay, Daddy," I assured him. Taking the phone off speaker, we caught up for the rest of the ride.

"I'm gonna let you go, Princess. I love y'all. You make sure to kiss my grandbaby for me too."

"I will, Daddy. And I love you more. I'll send pictures soon."

The automated system announced a minute left until the end of the call.

"Please do. Oh, and y'all follow instruction number three, aight?"

"Got it," I replied, and the call dropped. "He got a new phone, Grandma. He'll call from it once it's up and running." I relayed instruction number three to GNani.

"Okay."

We pulled up to GNani's building minutes later, and I was happy to see that my car was still parked and untouched. Melly helped her out the car and did the same for me and Amari. When I stepped out of the backseat, I moved a little slower than I intended. My body was still feeling the soreness from bringing life into the world.

"You movin' slow," he pointed out as I gripped the top of the car door. "You sure you should be driving?"

"No, she shouldn't," GNani answered for me. "She just hardheaded."

"I'm alright," I assured. "Just a little stiff. I can drive."

"We know that. The question is should you be driving?" Melly backed what GNani said. "I ain't doing shit till later. I can drive you home, Ma."

Sighing, I shifted my weight to my right side. By the looks

on their faces, it was clear that neither one was taking no for an answer. Instead of responding, I slid back in my seat.

"Well, shit, I love you too," GNani said as she turned away with her keys in her hand.

"I love you!" I yelled from the open door.

Melly laughed, strapping the baby back in.

"Y'all ain't have to double team me like that."

"Shiiddd, if we didn't, yo stiff ass would've been tryna whip that Audi with precious cargo. Sit back and relax. I'ma get you home, then I'ma be out of your way."

He did that winking shit again, and I had to roll my eyes to keep from smiling. *Ol' extra helpful, extra fine, young ass.*

ON THE RIDE TO MY PLACE, WE FELL INTO CONVERSATION instantly. He kept my interest the whole ride.

"This don't feel odd to you?"

"What? Being your Blankman?"

"Out of all of the superheroes, that's the one you picked?" I laughed.

Adjusting the visor so he could see me more, he smirked. "That's the Black one that I fuck wit."

"What you know about Blankman anyway?"

"Ahhh, here you go wit the young jokes. My aunt got a whole VHS player in her crib. I've seen the movie at least five times. And to answer your question, no. This doesn't feel odd to me."

"You must do this all the time then."

"Not at all. You just happened to catch me in the right staircase."

"Boy, shut up." I playfully mushed the back of his head.

"Nah, but forreal. I don't involve myself in people's business. I got love for GNani though. And you aight too."

"What do you do for a living?"

"I'm a barber."

"Really? I never knew that."

He laughed. "Who would've told you?"

"This is true. We don't run in the same circles. But look at us, in the same field. I own a beauty salon."

"Oh, word? That's wassup. How's that journey been? I'm in school now, working on my business degree. I wanna open my own spot."

"Being an entrepreneur has its ups and downs, but I love it. It was a pain in the ass in the beginning, if I'm being honest. Mainly because I didn't take the easy route and ask my father to front it for me. I got it out the mud forreal."

"Sound like you was on the type of time I'm on right now. I had to leave the shop I was working at. I made good money there, but I know what I can do on my own. I've seen it."

"And with drive like that, you can't be stopped."

I could hear the passion in his words, leading me to believe that nothing but good things would come from him going into business for himself. His drive made him even more attractive than his looks.

"I appreciate that. Real shit."

We got quiet for a second, and I figured I'd ask the question that had been burning in my mind the last couple days.

"The staircase, Melly?"

Glancing up in the mirror, he burst out laughing. "Ay, that shit was not planned. And it was a waste of my time. A nigga had to give too much guidance."

I shook my head. "She was so embarrassed."

"I don't know why. She the one who offered up her throat. I ain't ask. You still single?"

"Why? You want some of my throat too?" I said slickly.

Grinning, he shook his head. "I ain't even gon' go there witchu, shorty."

I snickered. "I don't know what you think changed over the

last two days, but yes, I'm still single. Single and focused. Am I correct to assume you are too?

He paused. "A lot can change in two days. As for me, I'm not committed to anybody. Been spending a lil' time with my ex though. Nothing serious, just really seeing if it's worth rekindling. Cimani's passing took a toll on both of us, so we're just figuring it out."

I nodded. "I get it."

"But again, still single. Still free to do me. Like who I wanna like."

We pulled up to my place, and he parked at the curb.

"Well, I'm not into breaking up happy homes, and you liking me ain't gon' change that, love. Like me from a distance. I don't need the drama."

Turning off the ignition, he turned back to me. "I said free to like who I wanna like, Ma. I ain't say free to like you."

My mouth dropped in embarrassment. It didn't help that he was staring at me with a straight face. No trace of a smile in sight.

"Oh… ummm… I…"

"Mannn," he cracked up, "I couldn't hold that shit in anymore. You know I like you, woman. I all but tell yo' fine ass that whenever I see you around. Come on so we can get the baby in the house."

Closing my mouth, I slowly got out of the car. I was stuck because why would he even play like that? He got my ass good. Humbled the fuck out of me.

I watched him grab the car seat like it was our practiced routine and follow me up to my door. Taking a step back, allowing me to open it, he walked inside behind me.

"Damn. It's warm in here," he let out as he set the car seat down.

"Let me put the air on."

"Oh, nah. Not the temperature. Warm like homely. Lived in. Peaceful. Shit feel like you was raised right."

"Thank you. I've never heard that compliment before."

"Rare breed, Ma. Rare breed."

Smiling, I agreed silently. "Thank you again. I owe you big time."

He nodded. "I know. You know what I'm about to say next, right?"

"Use your number if I need you. Got it."

"Be good, shorty. And you too, Amari."

I walked the few steps to the door and opened it for him. His lips curled into a slight grin before winking and casually bopping out to his car like he hadn't changed the whole course of my week and left a lasting impression.

I WAS GLAD THAT I HAD JALEN PUT AMARI'S ROOM TOGETHER months before I put him out. The last thing I wanted to do after birthing a whole human was play Bobiesha The Builder. Although it would be a couple months before I was comfortable with Amari sleeping in her room alone, knowing that all the heavy lifting was done put me at ease. Looking over at my little baby as she slept peacefully in her bassinet with one hand peeking out of the blanket I'd swaddled her in, my heart swelled.

It was our first night home, and the moment felt surreal. I was somebody's mama, responsible for her every waking moment and the protection when she was asleep. Hence the reason why I had her bassinet pulled into the living room with me. The TV was on, pretty much for background noise. While I glanced at it every now and then, I couldn't stop watching her. As my mind thought to wake her from her sleep just to see her beautiful smile, I heard my front door open. Stretching my neck so that I could see into the hallway, I could see Tamia juggling two shopping bags, a tote bag on her shoulder, and a tray with two drinks.

"Let me help you, girl." I giggled, getting up.

"Shit, I was about to say, 'Well, damn, can a bitch get a lil' help?'" She laughed, kicking the door closed with her foot. "Your alarm didn't go off."

"I know," I said, grabbing the two shopping bags from her hand and setting it. "I knew you were coming, so I didn't set it. You know that thing loud. Couldn't risk waking up the baby. Even though I wouldn't mind her getting up now."

"It smells like motherhood and good decisions in here, cousin. I already know you're doing a great job." Still laughing, she walked into the living room, setting the tote bag on the floor and the drinks on the coffee table. "I got you that mango green tea you like with the Boba at the bottom. And here's your keys." She handed me the keys and drink.

"Awww, thank you, boo. That was so sweet, Mia."

"No problem." She made her way over to the bassinet. "Awww, Happy Feet. Ya mama let yo step daddy drive y'all home." She cooed.

"Shut up." I playfully shoved her.

Turning to me, her eyes narrowed. "What? I'm just saying."

"Saying what?" I sat back down in my spot on the couch.

"Mr. Helpful been making himself available." Grabbing her drink, she kicked her shoes off and sat across from me.

"I know. And Grandma ain't making it no better, keep pawning me off on the man."

"Girl, can't nobody pawn you off. I think you like the attention. It's like a breath of fresh, young nigga air. I love that for you."

I snickered. "What the hell is young nigga air, Tamia?"

"Well," she sat back and crossed her legs, "it's usually polluted with loud, strip club wings, gunpowder, and bad decisions. It just depends on the young nigga. Melly's air smell like good dick, money, and good decision making. But he still got that dog in him. I can tell. What he like, twenty-three, twenty-four?"

"Twenty-five." I laughed. "And you stupid."

"Oh, twenty fine. Okay, okay. Even better. Shit, he got more sense than Jalen got at thirty-one. How the hell you miss the birth of your baby?" She sipped her tea, shaking her head.

"Likely somewhere fucking Toni when I called him."

"Excuse the fuck outta me?" Her neck jerked. "Toni? Your doula?"

"Yep. Ms. Mother Earth herself. I didn't tell you earlier, but he came by the hospital late. It was something about that damn Dior Sauvage that I couldn't get out of my head. And as sure as three plus three make six, he was fuckin' that bitch."

"That nigga really ain't got no code. Bitch, he is embarrassing. That lady done been in yo house. She assisted you in your birth plan. Fuck did he find sexy about that?"

"Girlll, niggas will find some shit. Maybe it was the bangles." We paused before bursting out laughing. "Nigga was under a spell." I made jokes to mask my disappointment in Jalen. "Forreal though, I let him know that there's some fuck ups you just can't take back. This is one of them."

Tamia nodded as silence fell over us. If anyone knew the ends and outs of what once was me and Jalen, it was her.

"Well, enough about him. Can I point out something without you gettin' how you get?"

Cocking my head to the side, my brows raised.

"Yeah, never mind." She waved her hand in the air and turned to the TV.

"No, say it. I'm not gonna get weird. Promise."

"Okay." She turned back quick, like she knew I'd come around. "You and Melly… there's an energy between the two of you. Something effortless. Easy."

"Girl, no, it is not. He's just a decent human that our grand-mother really adores. And this is the most we've ever talked besides when I see him around the way."

"Amariyah, you are probably the most safest person I know. Yet, you got in this man car, let him be in the hospital room when you pushed out your baby, and then he picked you up from the hospital. That ain't just no decent human being. That's a man who's watched you closely. Admired you from afar. I know what I'm talking about."

Grabbing a throw pillow, I set it in my lap for comfort. "He lost his daughter last year," I said softly. "She passed away at birth. Oddly, I felt like he needed that moment. That sounds crazy as hell, don't it?"

"No. It sounds like a connection. Sometimes, we don't know why people show up. They just come."

As I let her words sink in, my phone rang. It was Jalen call-ing. I held it up for her to see, and she gave it the finger.

Chuckling, I answered. **"Yeah?"**

"Hey." There was caution in his tone and for good reason. **"I know it's late. I was calling to see if you have a minute to talk?"**

"Amari is asleep."

"Huh?"

"Our daughter is asleep. And seeing as that's the only conversation I'm available for when it comes to you, there's nothing for us to talk about."

"Come on, Mari. After all the..."

"Bye, Jalen." I hung up and went to put the phone on DND when a text came through from Melly.

Melly: Y'all up?

I smiled before responding.

Me: I am. Amari is getting her beauty rest.

Melly: Oook. Don't forget babygirl's gift at
GNani crib. I'm not usually a good gift giver, but
I did a lil sum'n.

Me: 😊 it's the thought that counts.

Melly: Girl, that's what people say when they
don't like some shit. Don't it's the thought that
counts me. If you don't like it, I put a gift receipt
in the bag. You can take it back if anything.

Me: I won't but okay lol.

Melly: Whatever you say. I'll let you get back to
mommying. Have a goodnight, Ma.

Me: You too.

"It's the smiling and cheesing, cheesing and smiling fa me."
Tamia pointed out, sipping her drink.

"It's that young nigga air." I laughed, and we slapped fives.

I looked over the messages and felt a flutter in my stomach.
Connection. Something effortless. Easy. Maybe Tamia was on
to something with her assessment. Only time would tell.

6

MELLY

"And now, I'd like to call up our Valedictorian, Thomasina Jefferson, to address the graduating class." The principal of Innovation Charter high school introduced Teeny, and our whole row erupted.

Between Tanisha screaming her head off and my aunt with the airhorn, I knew for sure that we were about to be escorted off the premises. That shit was funny as hell. And it didn't faze Teeny a bit. She knew who her people were. Tanisha had come down from PA with her husband and my nieces. Our father had showed up a few minutes before the graduation started, ready to be front and center like he was on time. *I wanna be seen head ass.*

Tanisha was happy to see him, welcoming him with open arms. I managed to throw him a head nod after a nudge from Aunty Reece. My focus was on my sister though. Watching her walk confidently across the stage, cheeks full of pride with her cap and gown, was one of the proudest moments of my life next to being Cimani's father, even in her absence. My little sister was Valedictorian, the smartest in the whole school. Nobody was fucking with her in no shape or form.

Stepping up to the mic, she placed her hands on the podium and began a speech that she hadn't written down or let any of us hear beforehand.

"Ayeee, shoutout to God! The biggest to ever do it!" The high schoolers erupted in cheers and, as if they had rehearsed it, quieted down at the same time, making the families in the stands laugh. "No, seriously. We made it. From those sluggish walks down the halls after staying up all night studying for finals, to praying that Mrs. Kinglsey didn't hit us with a surprise quiz on our last full day, we made it. Don't just let this graduating moment be a moment in time. Let it continue to fuel your fire for all of your future endeavors. I'd like to thank my family for never letting me slack and always reminding me of the bigger picture. A special thanks to my brother, Jamel. Thank you for showing me what a hustler's spirit feels and looks like. You the real MVP. Valedictorian for the class of 2025, over and out!"

She finished her speech with the *I'm So ATL* dance while walking off the stage as her peers rapped the lyrics. I clapped so loud behind the woman's head who sat in front of me; I could hear her mumble her dissatisfaction to a man who sat next to her. I didn't give a fuck. My sister had just called me the MVP. They lucky I ain't get to running across the field.

After the ceremony, we took a thousand and two pictures with Teeny posing with enough balloons to fly off with.

"How y'all fit all these balloons in the car with the kids?" I asked Tanisha as I slapped one out of my face after the pictures.

"Marcus fought to put them in the trunk because I wasn't leaving without them," she responded while laughing.

"Watched me like a hawk to make sure we ain't lose one," he added, shaking his head.

Their one-year-old twins were knocked out in their stroller. The heat coupled with the noise from the crowd had taken a toll on them.

"How bout we all do lunch to celebrate?" my father suggested. "On me."

"That sounds nice," my Aunt Reece let out, and Tanisha agreed like I knew she would.

"No offense, Dad, but I'm good," Teeny said, shifting the balloons, so he could see her face. "The only celebrating I'm looking to do is moving my stuff into Melly's place before he changes his mind."

"Mann," I chuckled, "why you keep tryna put me on the spot? I already said you good."

My father gave me that fake look of concern that was really a mask for judgement, one that I'd seen a few times from him throughout the years. Only I gave a fuck less now than I did a few years ago.

"You think that's a good idea, Reece? I mean, you've been her primary guardian since she was little. Did I miss something?"

"You didn't miss anything, Mel," my aunt replied, while I chose to stay silent for the sake of her. "Teeny's getting older, and she can make decisions. Melly's got her."

"I hear you, but the boy has got a lot going on already. He needs to focus on where he's headed before taking on more responsibility."

My jaw tightened and flexed before I spoke. "I don't know what boy you talkin' bout, but I'm a grown ass man. You don't know what a nigga got going on forreal. And unlike you, just cause Teeny been living with Aunty don't mean she ain't been my responsibility."

"I'm just saying you're a bachelor, son. I'm sure you're keeping crazy hours. The last time we spoke, you said you were locked in with school and cutting. How you gon' have time to look after her?"

Teeny didn't miss the opportunity to interject on my behalf. "Nobody has to look after me, Dad. I'm not a kid."

"I know that, Teeny…"

"Hol' up," I cut in. "You out here tryna speak on my life like I don't have the time for my sister when the truth is... Nigga, you don't have the time to be a father. How is it that you acknowledge that she been with Aunty Reece for years, yet she ain't never spent more than a week with you? As far as I'm concerned, you and that lady who gave birth to us are one in the same. Only difference is she don't fake like she fuck wit us."

Everyone went quiet as we stood a couple feet away, staring each other down. Sure, this wasn't the time for me to spill my inner feelings, but this nigga had me fucked up. And I was gonna deal with disrespect wherever the offense occurred.

"Okay, let's just relax and remember where we are." Tanisha slid in, trying to play mediator like she always did.

"And here you go wit that *keep the peace* bullshit. Instead of holding this nigga accountable, you always want somebody to calm down. No. I'm not walkin' on eggshells around this nigga."

"I ain't gon' be too many more niggas, Jamel," he warned.

I ain't know who he thought that deep voice shit was scaring. "Shiiidd, you can be a bi..."

"Jamel!" My aunt stopped me from calling him a bitch ass nigga. "You made your point, nephew. Let it go."

Out of the pure respect I had for her, I turned and started toward the exit. I could hear my sisters calling out my name, catching up to me as I made it to the street.

"Melly, we got on heels. Wait a damn minute!" Tanisha yelled out in frustration.

"What?" I turned to the both of them.

"Why you gotta be like that? We supposed to be celebrating, not fighting with each other."

"Why you over here talking to me about it, Toot?" I called her by her nickname. "Talk to yo father. That nigga spoke on me. I ain't speak on him."

"And I am gonna talk to him, but you the one who walked away."

"Would you rather he have stayed?" Teeny questioned. "You know our brother don't got it all. And once he get going, ain't no stopping him."

"That's what I'm saying, twin." I agreed with her assessment of me.

"Every time y'all get around each other, it don't have to be an issue though. That's our father."

"Jay-Z is Blue Ivy's father."

"What?"

"Shit, I thought since we were throwing out facts that I don't give a fuck about, I'd throw out my own."

Teeny giggled, and Tanisha sucked her teeth.

"I'm being serious, Melly."

"Me too."

Sighing, she shook her head. "I give up. I'ma leave it alone… this time. But we need to have a sit down."

"No, **we** don't." Reaching out, I pulled her into a hug. "I love you."

"I love you too. And you too, Teeny." They embraced for a few seconds before pulling back.

"Don't be talking about us at dinner either, Toot," Teeny said while wagging a finger at her. "All for one and one for all, like you used to say growing up."

"Always. Call me whenever y'all get to where y'all going."

"Aight."

She walked off, leaving me and Teeny watching her back.

Turning to me, Teeny smiled. "Brunch?"

"Hell yeah. But I ain't fighting with them balloons. So, you gotta figure that out."

"Bet."

Like two peas in a pod, we went off to do our own thing. Nothing or no one was gonna stop me from celebrating my sister.

We ended up at a brunch spot out in Queens that Teeny found on TikTok. The drive was longer than I'd expected it to be. She was lucky it was her graduation day, and I was letting her have it her way. We walked into Sunday Soul, a small spot that gave off a family vibe. R&B tunes played through the speakers, and the smell of homemade biscuits and jam hit my nose immediately. Rubbing my hands together like Birdman, I was ready to grub.

"What you getting?" I asked Teeny, who was so occupied with recording the place that she hadn't looked at the menu.

"I want the stuffed French toast with strawberry compote that I saw on their page. I think it comes with scrambled eggs and sausage."

"Put the phone down and pick up the menu so you can see, Teeny."

Giggling, she set her phone down on the table. "You right. You right."

I shook my head and did the same. "I'ma get the chicken and waffles with a side of hash browns."

"Okay. I'm ready to order."

The waitress came over to take our drink and food orders and tried to do a little flirting in between. A nigga was hungry as hell, so all that shit was going over my head. And I wouldn't be me if I didn't let her know that.

"Shorty, no offense. And if you get offended, please don't come out the side of ya neck cause I'm known to be one rude ass nigga. You cute and all, but can you flirt when you bring the check? I'm hungry as hell, and I just came to eat and celebrate my lil sister here." I pointed over at Teeny, who wasn't the least bit fazed by how brash I was.

The waitress snatched the menus up and scurried off.

"She should've cussed you out." Teeny laughed while scrolling her phone.

"Then you would've had to fight on your big brother's behalf."

"Tore her right on up in my good clothes."

She gave me a pound.

"So, what you bringing over from Aunty house?"

"Wellll," she dragged, "I was just gonna bring my clothes. Because I figured my big brother would let me decorate my new room to my liking."

"Oh, you did?"

She nodded. "Yeah. And I can ball on a budget. Am I getting the spare room that has the bathroom in it?"

"Yeah. Figured it would make sense. And we can get you some stuff to decorate. I want you to be comfortable in yo shit, so you can stay outta my shit. What about your clients? I don't want nobody in my crib."

"I figured that. I'm gonna see if Aunty lets me take my regulars at the house still, and I'll travel for new clients."

Teeny was a self-taught nail tech. At first, it was a hobby, but she took to it immediately, and like me with the clippers, she had been building a name for herself. She'd successfully completed her course hours a couple months ago and secured her license. Another proud moment.

"Not too sure on the travel. I have something in mind though. Let me work on it." I thought about Amariyah and the shop she owned.

"Okay."

Our food and drinks were brought out to us twenty minutes later, this time by a different waitress. The other was clearly offended by what I said. Teeny said grace, and we dug in.

"So, have you heard from Amariyah?"

"A couple times. You know ya brother don't do too much."

"You like her though. Been liking her. You need to do the most."

I hid my grin behind glass as I took a sip of my orange juice. "Can't come on too strong, T. She just had a baby and shit. Plus, I'm still fucking with Paige."

"I know. The things that make you go hmmmm."

Chuckling, I soaked my waffle in syrup and took a bite. "What you mean?"

"Nothing really. Just wondering why you're spinning that block when you know for a fact that you don't see a future with Paige. You did at one point, but…." She paused and looked down at her plate, avoiding my eyes.

"Speak your mind, twin," I encouraged.

"I feel like losing Cimani broke something so deep within the two of you that trying to be back together would just remind y'all of what y'all lost. I don't think it's healthy. Especially since she refuses to seek the help she needs to deal with her grief in a way that's conducive to the people around her."

I sat back in my seat and stared at my seventeen-year-old sister spitting some real shit. She was spot on with her assessment. I went to say something when my phone vibrated in my pocket. Taking it out, a text notification from Paige popped up on the screen. Opening the notification, I sighed.

Paige: You should be a magician the way you do these disappearing acts. At this point, we just need to call it what it is. We tried taking things slow to get back to us, but I don't think it's in the cards.

Me: I think you're right.

Paige: ….okay.

Her response let me know that she didn't expect me to agree.

But after what Teeny had just said, I knew I had to keep it real with not just Paige but myself.

I ran my hand down my face and shook my head. Paige didn't know how to deal with her emotions, so I didn't know why I expected any response other than the one she gave.

Exiting our thread, a text came through from Amariyah.

My brows furrowed, confused as to what she was talking about. Then, it dawned on me. My assignment for my business class was due by 5 p.m.

The last we'd talked during the week, I'd sent her an assignment I was working on to get her feedback. She was eager to help out, saying it reminded her of when she was in school working toward her business degree.

Me: Preciate you. I'll hit you once I leave here. Have you eaten anything?

Mari: Just a fruit salad. Nothing major. But stop texting me and focus on the graduate. Tell her I said congrats🩶.

I sent a thank you response and locked my phone. Looking up, Teeny was staring right at me.

"What, man?"

Smiling, she took a bite of her French toast. "I ain't say nothing, Kool-Aid Man."

Ignoring her, I finished up my food. We stayed at the restaurant another hour before leaving and going on an impromptu shopping trip for her new room. We made a deal that I would buy her a new bedroom set, vanity, and mini fridge, while she took care of her wall art, bedding, and whatever else made the space hers.

I was about to be big bro/roommate with a teenager. We hadn't lived in the same house for some time, so I expected an adjusting period. And I was cool with it. Especially for my twin.

7

AMARIYAH

My phone lit up beside me, vibrating against the throw pillow on the couch. I'd just put Amari down after taking two trips around the living room, rocking her to sleep. Today, my one-week-old had me going. Between diaper changes, feedings, and staring at each other, trying to figure out what was next, the day had flown by.

Checking the phone, I smiled at the screen when I saw Melly's name before unlocking it.

> Melly. My stomach was growling, and I thought about you.

> Me: Lol. What?

> Melly: 😒 have you eaten anything since that fruit you told me about earlier?

I chewed my lip, realizing I hadn't. My stomach didn't feel it either. I made sure I was hydrated though. Had to stay hydrated for a continuous flow of titty milk.

Me: I haven't. I've been at Amari's beck and
call.

Melly: We gotta fix that. You mind if I bring you
something?

My stomach fluttered, and it had nothing to do with hunger. I wanted to see him again. And a man that wanted to feed me was a man I wanted to be around. I peeked over at Amari, who was still asleep, and sent a text back.

Me: I could eat.

Melly: Me too.

Me: Omg! Melly! Lmao.

His flirting made me shift on the couch.

Melly: Just putting it out there. What you in the
mood for though?

Me: Ummm. Ooouuu, Indian food. There's a
spot close to my house that's really good. Wait,
how far out are you?

Melly: I'm at my crib in White Plains.

Me: That's a two-hour drive, Melly. You talking
like you around the corner. I can DoorDash it.

Melly: Shiiiddd. Last time we spoke was earlier
this morning. You ain't ate since then. What's
another two hours?

I laughed out loud because his statement was true. He was such a smart ass.

Me: You know what, smart ass? Come on. I'm
gonna send you my order, and if you miss
anything, I'ma send you right back to the store.

Melly: And when I get everything right, you do
me a favor.

I paused before responding. Technically, I did owe him a favor, but I didn't want him making it weird. But at the same time, he didn't give me weird vibes. I agreed and hoped for the best.

Me: Deal.

Melly: Bet. Send me the name of the place and
your order.

———

By the time he sent a text letting me know he had picked up the food, I'd fed and changed Amari once more and put her back down to sleep. In just a week's time, I had her schedule down to a science. GNani had been encouraging me to sleep when she slept, and I took the advice to the point where I wasn't delirious due to lack of sleep but knew I could use more. I straightened the living room up just enough to make it feel like it hadn't been overrun by newborn chaos.

I traded my mumu for a grey two-piece pajama set that gave mom but still cute. My phone went off again, and this time, Melly had texted that he was outside. Walking over to the door, I opened it to him holding up a brown paper bag, flashing a half-smile.

"Wassup?" he spoke smoothly, pulling me in for a hug that I didn't expect.

"Hey," I said with a toothy grin. "Come in."

Stepping inside, he held the bag up. "Now, you ain't offer a nigga no food, but I got enough for us to share. That cool?"

I sucked my teeth playfully. "I was gonna share with you anyway," I said, walking toward the kitchen. "You ever had Indian food?"

"Nah. But this shit smell good as fuck. Where baby girl?"

"In the living room, sleep."

"Can I see her?"

"Yeah."

I took the food from him. He hiked up his shorts and bopped into the living room. This whole T-shirt and sweat-short combo he rocked was doing it for me. His locs were in four plats, showing off every tattoo on his neck. I watched as he peeked inside of Amari's bassinet, stared for a few seconds, then headed back my way.

"Yo baby gon' have hands when she get older. She sleep like she ready for the bullshit."

I laughed because my baby really slept like she was on guard. "I know. My baby don't fuck around." I opened the brown bag, and the smell of Garlic Naan permeated the air. "Ughhh. I can't wait to eat. I wasn't able to eat Indian food my whole pregnancy."

"Why?"

"It gave me the worst heartburn. But babyyyy, we back!" I took out each labeled container and set it on the counter. Leaning back against the counter, I folded my arms. "Okay, what's the favor?" I asked, admitting that he'd gotten everything I ordered right without saying it out loud.

He smirked. "Well, first, you can start by admitting that I got the order right."

Flashing him a lazy smile, I tilted my head. "I did."

"I must've missed it."

"Oh, my God." I laughed. "You got the order right. Now, what's the favor? And it better not be nothing crazy," I warned.

"My lil' sister, Teeny. She a nail tech and shit. Been doing nails out my aunt crib for the last three years. Now that she's moving in with me, she wanna step it up. I don't want her traveling to other peoples' houses and shit. So, I was wondering if you could plug her in somewhere. You know, wit you being in the beauty industry and all."

My heart melted as I listened to him speak about his sister. The gleam in his eyes didn't go unnoticed. "Let me see her work. If she got some skills, I'd be happy to set her up on a trial run at my shop. Does she do acrylics? Right now, I just have a manicurist. I'd love to have someone young who can do the trending sets that the girlies come in and ask for."

"Shorty, I've paid for plenty nail sets, but I don't know the lingo. Here, lemme show you her IG." Taking out his phone, he tapped the screen a couple times and handed it to me.

TeeDidThat was the Instagram page, and just by the first couple posts, I was sold that she knew what she was doing. The content was clean, letting me know she took pride in her work. The first pinned post was a picture of her as well as an About Me, which I loved. She was so pretty. She and Melly favored each other around the eyes and nose.

Clicking on her booking link, I skimmed it for any unnecessary rules. The beauty industry was different now. There were rules for the rules, and that shit was irritating to say the least. Everything was clear cut on her page. Deposit rules and methods of payment, scheduling, specifics on how to book, and a contact number for questions. Clear and concise.

"And she's seventeen?" I asked, not believing the age she posted in her About Me.

"Yeah. Going on thirty-seven. She's organized as hell and professional."

I handed him back the phone. "I'm out on maternity leave for a few weeks, but I'm gonna reach out to the manager to arrange a meet at the shop. Just send me her contact before you leave. I'm gonna follow her on IG too."

"Good looking. I appreciate it."

"Of course. That was an easy favor," I said, taking the tops off the food and grabbing two plates.

"What you thought? I was gon' ask to fuck or sum'n?"

I nodded. "Or for a lil' throat. You know how you do."

We both laughed.

"You ain't gon' let me live that down, huh?"

"I need about another week, and I'll be done. You wanna try a little of everything?" I asked, pointing to the spread of Butter chicken, Tiki Marsala, Naan bread, veggie and lamb Samosas.

"The people at the spot recommended starting off with the Butter chicken and the Naan since I'm a beginner."

I plated the chicken, making sure to put the Naan bread on a different dish for him to taste separately. "Drink? I have ginger ale, water, and tropical punch juice."

"I'll take a ginger ale."

Grabbing a bottle for the both of us out of the fridge, I handed him his. "Let's go into the living room. That way, I can keep an eye on Amari."

Taking a seat across from each other, me closer to Amari, we ate in silence for a few minutes. A comfortable silence. Again, I felt like we'd done this before.

"How was your day?" he asked.

"It was cool. Caught up on all my shows. Did a little laundry and hung out with my homegirl." I nodded toward Amari's bassinet. "She's great company. A good listener."

He chuckled. "I bet she is."

"How bout yours?"

"It was good. I had to tell my dad about himself after the graduation, but I didn't let it stop me from celebrating Teeny. I took her out to eat after, then we went shopping for her room.

At this point, I'm convinced that she wants to see just how much money I have."

"She's just a girl," I said in her defense. "That sucks that you got into it with your father. Especially on such a big day. Was Teeny mad?"

"Nah, my older sister was though. Talkin' that time and place shit."

"You don't believe that there's a time and place for conflict?"

He set his plate down on the table and took a sip of his soda. "I'll put it to you like this. If I'm at the pearly gates bout to see what the vibes are in Heaven and a nigga say something crazy to me, he gon' have to see me right then and there."

"So, you have a temper?"

"I wouldn't say that. I just move a certain way, and I have zero tolerance for disrespect. I don't go fuckin' wit people, and I don't like to be fucked wit."

"That's fair."

"I also don't have as much patience as I could. I'll admit that that's something I need to work on."

"You should. Especially since you'll be having a young adult living with you."

"Mannn, don't remind me." He swiped his hand over his face. "Ion know what I'ma do when I start walking in to her making her TikToks."

"And trying to include you in them." I giggled. "You gotta be a good sport and do at least one. You can really make the content work as promotion for you."

"Remind me to not bring her around you. I can already see the wheels turning in your head."

I laughed and went to explain the pros of how being on social media could help him going into business for himself. Before I could, I was cut off by the ringing of my doorbell. Melly looked over at it with a raised brow. He turned so that his body was fully facing the door, while I got up to answer it.

"One second." Walking over to it, I looked through the peephole and was surprised to see Jalen standing on my porch.

Opening the door, I stood against it. "Hey."

"Hey," he replied, energy off.

"Wassup, Jalen?" I pushed.

"Whose car is that parked in the driveway next to yours?"

"My friend's, Jalen. Wassup? What you doing here?"

"Came by to see Amari."

"She's asleep, and I have company. Come back tomorrow. A little earlier is preferred. And you need to call before you just pop up at my house."

His eyes narrowed as he tried to look around me. "You got a nigga in there?"

"I have company," I repeated with irritation laced in my tone.

"Oh, word? You lettin' niggas around our daughter?!" His voice rose. "It ain't even been a week, and you doing it like that?"

"First off, lower your voice and act like you have a little class. Second, I'm not doing it like nothing. Who I have in the house **I** pay for is none of your concern. Amari is safe, so that's not something you have to worry about. Again, you are welcome to visit your daughter tomorrow. During the day. Have a blessed night."

"Aight. I see the typa time you on. Say less. I'll be back."

"During the day," I said to his back as he turned to leave.

I watched as he hopped in his car, slammed the door, and sped off. Shaking my head, I closed my door and locked it. Embarrassed to face Melly, I slowly made my way back to the living room.

"You want me to beat yo baby daddy ass?" he asked from the couch.

The question was so random, I burst out laughing. "Melly, no."

"You sure? I thought I was gon' have to violate that nigga soon as he asked who was in here. Then, I thought about that whole *time and place* thing."

"I appreciate that. Thank you."

"Nah. Thank baby girl. Had she not been here, all that shit would've went out the window."

I didn't know how to respond. I just knew I was turned the fuck on. Cause yeah, be ready to crash out bout me and it's only been a week.

"You still up for chilling, or you need me to leave?" he asked, pulling me from my thoughts.

"I'm cool with you staying. So long as you're comfortable."

"Why wouldn't I be? You think that nigga gon' come back? Cause I got somethin' to make him lay down," he sang.

"No. Crazy. Oouuu, I have an idea." Grabbing a notebook from the kitchen drawer, I sat back in my seat on the couch. "Let's put your business plan together," I said excitedly.

He stared at me a few seconds before his lips parted into a smile. "You don't wanna watch a movie, play Uno, Checkers, or nothing like that? You wanna work on a business plan at nine in the evening, shorty?"

"Nigga, hustlas don't stop. They keep goinnn!" I mimicked Young Thug.

We laughed out loud, and Amari whimpered.

"You better keep it down fore baby Ali wake up," he whispered.

I peeked over in her bassinet, expecting her eyes to flutter open, but they didn't.

"Okay, we're good. You ready?"

"Yeah."

For the remainder of the night, we talked about his plans to start off with a barber suite. Surprisingly, he knew more than I thought, even pulled out his phone to show me the numbers he'd crunched to make it happen. By the time he left my house, not only was I impressed by the way his brain worked, but I was absolutely smitten by the man.

8

MELLY

The past few weeks had been good to a young nigga soul forreal. Although busy, it was all for the right reasons. Since coming up with a solid business plan, my clientele had doubled. Between cutting, adjusting to life with my new roommate, juggling assignments for this last semester, and just continuing to be a real nigga, I didn't know whether I was coming or going sometimes.

Then there was Amariyah.

She was the balance. Amariyah had found a way to fit into my life without forcing it. The way her presence had naturally become a part of my day to day had me feeling like I'd met **the one**. If someone were to ask how it happened, I wouldn't even know what to tell them. We'd unknowingly fallen into a routine.

If we weren't chillin' at her place, watching Amari discover new ways to get out of that baby cocoon Amariyah had her wrapped in, we were on FaceTime. Our FaceTime dates often consisted of her quizzing me on assignments, while she walked around with the baby propped up on her shoulder. She'd even gotten comfortable enough to where she would breastfeed with me on the line — covered of course. Although I did catch a glimpse of side titty a time or two that I wasn't mad at.

Spending time this way made it easy for us to get to know each other without limits. We just worked around the schedule. And most importantly, we respected each other's time, even with Amari's father popping in and out like the proudest absentee father alive. I could tell that it bothered Amariyah, but, in her mind, she was being the bigger person. I hated it for her, but it wasn't my place to speak on it… yet. It felt like we were getting to that point though.

She had even met Teeny last week. They vibed instantly on FaceTime, talking and cracking jokes like they'd been friends for years. Teeny had officially started at her salon and had been fitting right in with the ladies. She had an old soul, so I wasn't surprised.

"You sure you got everything?" I asked Amariyah, taking a sip of my Gatorade.

I leaned against the edge of my counter with my phone propped up, watching her move around her bedroom. Today was Amari's six-week checkup, and with the way she was darting back-and-forth, one would've thought she was running late to her own wedding. While she added more than enough clothes, bibs, diapers, and other baby essentials into the diaper bag, the baby was laid across the bed, fighting the air.

"I think so." She finally stopped to answer, half-distracted. "Insurance card, diapers, wipes, extra clothes, bottles… Damn, I should probably pump for one more bottle."

"Breathe, baby," I encouraged.

"I am breathing, Jamel," she replied. "If they didn't change her pediatrician at the last minute, I probably wouldn't be so all over the place."

"Take a minute. It's just her six-week checkup, remember? Not her first day of daycare. You got everything. Look." I held up the checklist I'd taken the liberty of making her the night before when she mentioned the appointment. "I checked off everything as you put it in the bag."

Leaning into the camera, she flashed an appreciative smile. "I see why the girls give they throat to you. Thank you so much."

"Girl, get the baby and get to the car." I laughed. Amariyah didn't know it, but every time she hinted at something sexual, it let me know that she really wanted to be on that type of time with a nigga. I was still following her lead.

Strapping Amari into her car seat, she held it in the crook of her arm. With the baby bag on her shoulder, she headed for the door. I could hear her doorbell ring before she got there.

"I hope this ain't Jalen," she mumbled. "I am not in the mood today. Hold on, Melly." The screen went black, but I could still hear.

"Hi, Amariyah Baker?" I could hear a man's voice clearly.

"Yeah?" she replied.

"You've been served," he said flatly. The call went silent.

Served? I thought. "Hello? Hello?"

"Gimme a second." I could hear what sounded like something being ripped open. "Oh, no this bitch ass nigga didn't," she said out loud. There was a pause before I could see her face again.

"Wassup? What's wrong?"

She didn't answer at first, but I could see her eyes glossing over in disbelief. "Jalen is taking me to court for joint custody. He's tryna take my baby from me, Jamel."

"Aye, I'm on my way." Snatching my keys off the counter, I headed for the front door.

"No. I'm okay." She blinked back tears. "We can't miss this appointment."

"Send me the address and I'll meet you there. Either way, I'm coming."

"Okay." She didn't put up a fight. "I'll text it to you."

"Aight. Mari," I called out before I hung up.

"Yes?" she replied with a look of defeat that I didn't like at all.

"That nigga ain't taking Happy Feet, you hear me?"

She nodded.

"Nah. Say that shit so I know you know what I know."

"He not taking Happy Feet."

"Send the addy."

Ending the call, I hopped in the car with a one-track mind. I had to get to my girls.

PULLING INTO THE PARKING LOT OF THE PEDIATRICIAN'S OFFICE, I hopped out of my car ready to take it there about my lil' family that you couldn't tell me wasn't mine. Me and Amariyah weren't official, but what was understood about what we were developing didn't need to be explained. Per her text instructions, if I couldn't find the office once I entered the building, I was to follow the people with strollers and crying babies. I did just that, following behind a couple with a double stroller, and entered the office.

My eyes scanned the room to find Amariyah seated near the receptionist desk with her phone in one hand and Amari clutched to her chest, rocking her. I recognized Amari's cries amongst the other little ones in the room and made a beeline to her. As if she could sense me near, Amariyah looked up, eyes tight with stress.

"Hey," she breathed out, standing and shifting Amari to her other shoulder.

I embraced her, pulling her into my body, careful not to squeeze the baby. Placing a kiss on her forehead, I took Amari from her arms. As she pulled away, I could tell she didn't know how to respond to my gesture. I didn't trip. Though we flirted heavily and shared intimate moments, we'd never done anything remotely sexual.

"I'm here," I assured her as I rubbed Amari's back. She quieted down as soon as I got her. Her little body curled up on my shoulder.

"How did I know she was gonna do that?"

I smirked. "You know this my lil' mama."

"No. I think it's because you spoil her so bad," she countered.

"That too. How long she been fussing like that?"

"Whole ride here," she muttered. "I fed her. Burped her. Her diaper empty. All should be right with the world."

"Except it ain't. The most important person ain't right. You. She's feeling your frustration."

I watched her head slowly fall and caught it with my finger just before it hit her chest. "Yeah, we not doing that, Ma. We not doing that shit at all. You ca…"

I was cut off by a nurse calling Amari's name.

"Come on," she said, grabbing the diaper bag. "And watch how she start showing out as soon as you put her down."

"Tell Mommy don't worry bout us, lil' mama," I said to Amari.

We followed the nurse to the back where I handed Amari off to be weighed and measured. And just as Amariyah predicted, she wasn't having it, fussing the whole way through. A solid eight pounds, she was on track with her length and reflexes.

"It's okay, baby. It's okay," the nurse cooed while checking her ears. "You can pick her up now, Mommy. The doctor will be right in," she said to Amariyah once she was done. "She's perfect, by the way."

"Thank you," we both said at the same time.

The nurse laughed before leaving the room. Amariyah wrapped the baby in her receiving blanket and cuddled her.

"She ain't feeling this at all." I pointed out. "You think it's too cold in here for her? Maybe she don't like the environment." I looked around the Minnie and Mickey Mouse themed room.

"She's not even holding her own bottle yet. She don't know

anything about the environment, Melly." She shook her head, smiling.

"Shit. Remember what GNani said bout them post COVID babies."

A knock at the door caught our attention. Amariyah gave the okay to enter, and the pediatrician walked in. She was an older, Black woman with long dreads pushed back from her face by a headband.

"Hello, all," she greeted cheerfully. "And who is the special visitor here today?"

"This is Amari," Amariyah replied, turning the baby so that she was facing the doctor.

"Oh, my goodness. Look at this cutie with these chunky legs," she cooed, making Amari blow spit bubbles. "I'm just gonna do a quick check. I know it gets a little chilly in here, and our babies don't go for that at all."

"That's what I said," I uttered.

The doctor grinned. "Any concerns?" she asked while sanitizing her hands.

"Not at all," Amariyah confirmed. "She's really perfect. I mean, today she was a little fussy until this guy came in."

"Yeah. They say dads are baby whisperers. You can put her right here on the table." While the doctor did her examination, I watched from my seat as she and Amariyah talked.

It was the second time I'd been referred to as dad since Amari had been born. The first time was my doing, of course, but she never corrected me. I wasn't trippin' about it, but I did want to know how she felt. There was no question of who Amari's dad was when it came to her birth certificate. But the nigga having the title of father was questionable seeing as he didn't show up as one.

"So, no shots today?" Amariyah questioned, and I sat up for the response.

I didn't like hearing Amari cry. Hence why she was so

spoiled. Even on FaceTime, if I heard her whimper, I would give Amariyah a look that said, *pick my baby up.*

"Not today," the doctor confirmed, making me breathe easy. "But there are some vaccines at the two-month mark."

"What if she don't want them?" I asked seriously.

They gave each other inquisitive looks before laughing.

"The vaccines are for preventative care," the doctor assured. "We want to make sure our little ones are protected."

I looked down at the baby and made a face. "We'll discuss it later and see what you think, lil' mama."

"And when you do, be sure to get back to me with an answer," the doctor joked. "We're all set. See you soon, Amari." She left the room, and Amariyah shook her head at me, smiling.

"What?"

"Nothing. You're just… something else." She pulled Amari's dress over her head and placed her back in the car seat.

"In a good way?"

"A great way."

"Okay, cool. You wanna grab something to eat? I know how you feel about being out with her, but some air would do her some good. You too."

Her face said she wanted to object, then she sighed. "Yeah. I could use a drink."

My brow raised. "A drink?"

"Yes. Maybe two. I have milk stored for times like this."

"Times like what?"

Strapping Amari in, she grabbed the diaper bag and looked up at me with a straight face. "Times where I have to be reminded that I have a life to live for so I can't take another."

She didn't blink when she spoke. Instead, there was a fire in her eyes that made a nigga dick hard as fuck. What the fuck was this woman doing to me?

⸻

WE ENDED UP AT A CARIBBEAN-INDIAN FUSION SPOT THAT WASN'T too far from her place. I opted to sit outside on the patio, away from the small crowd inside. Didn't want to have a whole bunch of people around her. She convinced me to order the jerk lamb over rice, while she ordered oxtails and roti.

"How is it that I've been living here a few years and didn't know about this place?" she asked as she pulled the net over Amari's car seat to shield her from the sun.

"You know a young nigga gotta show you things you've never seen."

"Boy, please." She smirked, leaning forward. "And who told you about it?"

I met her in the middle of the table where we were close enough to touch noses. "TikTok," I said confidently before pecking her nose and sitting back.

"That was smooth."

"I know," I replied cockily.

Our food didn't take long to come, and she ordered two well deserved drinks. Watching her relax, even if it were just for a little while, felt good. We talked about everything but Jalen and the court papers. The whole point of the outing was to get her mind off the bullshit. In the middle of eating, her phone rang. Picking it up, she smiled.

"One sec. It's my father."

"Do ya thang." I continued eating, while she took her call.

I knew of Prince from the stories in the hood. He had a good rep for being solid. He was Amariyah's world too. The way she spoke on his name showed just how much she loved, respected, and honored the man.

"Okay, Daddy, but he might not wanna talk to you. Alright, I'ma put you on speakerphone, so you can hear him." She held the phone to her chest. "He wants to talk to you, but if you don't want to, you don't have to."

Smirking, I caught her drift. She was lowkey telling me to

say I didn't want to talk. But I wasn't running from no man. "Give me the phone, shorty."

"It's…"

I chuckled. "It's cool. I'll talk to him."

She slowly handed the phone over, and I put it to my ear. **"Hello?"**

"Wassup, Melly? How you?"

"I'm good. Maintaining. How bout yourself?"

"Shit, playing the cards I was dealt. I just wanted to speak to the man that's been making my daughter's days a little lighter. Preciate you for stepping in the way you have. Not a lot of young men out here doing that. Especially not with anyone they haven't locked in with yet. That's honorable of you."

Amariyah pretended to be busy with her food, but I could see her glance up every now and then.

"She makes it easy to be an honorable man. And we locked in. If she didn't know it before, she knows now."

He chuckled. **"Sounds like she done pulled her a me. I like your approach. Keep that energy. Talk soon."**

"Copy. Hold ya head." I handed her back the phone and let her finish her conversation uninterrupted.

Once the call ended, she set her fork down and stared at me. "Locked in, huh?"

"Like a motherfucka. I don't know if you noticed, but a nigga don't see nobody but you. You and Amari have become a part of me. When I get up in the morning, I think about y'all. When I rest my head at night and send those prayers up to God to keep my people safe, I include y'all. I know she not mine by blood, but when I hear someone refer to me as her pops, my heart swells with pride. You don't know what you've done to a nigga life in such a short time, Amariyah. You always thanking me for being there for you, not even knowing how easy you make it to show up. I'm gonna continue to show up for y'all. Only now, I want it to be full time."

What came next wasn't planned, but it happened like the most natural thing in the world. We moved in sync, leaning over the table. Our lips met for the first time, our tongues speaking every unspoken thought. The way she sucked on my lip made me want to tear her ass up right then and there for the world to see. She pulled back first, licking her lips.

"Just so you know, I'm either a stalker or uninterested, baby. Ain't no in between with me. In other words, I can be on yo' ass or it's fuck ya. So, if you gon' lock in with a nigga, lock in."

"My body's been wanting you for a while now. But it's my mind and heart that's been craving your presence when you're not around. Once I give you access to either, it's over for what you think you can handle when it comes to me. There's no half stepping. You have to continue to give it your all and then some. I'm not a snack, Melly. I'm a full course meal. The wine that's not on the menu. I'm that shit you gotta request before you get to the establishment. Very exclusive. Continue what you're doing and then some."

"Fuck wit a young nigga, and I'ma show you sum'n. You won't regret it."

She nodded with a smirk. I planned to show her better than I ever could tell her.

9

AMARIYAH

nn Marie's *It's Given* played at a low volume in the car as me and Amari made our way to GNani's. I was running on four hours of sleep, but my body felt like I'd gotten a good ten. I didn't feel sluggish. My eyelids weren't heavy. And as I'd passed the manilla folder on my kitchen counter that contained the custody petition, I didn't feel the least bit worried.

I felt light. And I was sure that it had everything to do with Melly. He was the first thing that crossed my mind when I cracked my eyes open this morning. He hadn't even stayed the night. But the memory of him had settled into my couch where we'd cuddled for hours after putting Amari to bed. There was something innocent but yet intimate about the cuddling. From the way he rubbed the small of my back to the way he palmed my booty when commenting on how round it was, it was everything I wanted but didn't expect.

Melly made his intentions clear. He wanted to lock in. And if that wasn't enough, him getting on the phone with my father told me everything I needed to know. I'd given him an out by prewarning him, yet he stepped up, taking the call on his grown man shit. I openly listened to his tone for any hesitance and found none. His voice was calm but firm and respectful. People were often intimated by my father's reputation alone, but the way his body relaxed in the chair showed he wasn't.

When he handed the phone back, my father's words before ending the call were, *"I wanna meet him."* He'd never said that about Jalen, but he always told me that when I had someone worth meeting, he'd let me know. I guess Melly was that someone.

I pushed Amari's stroller up the ramp to GNani's building, praying that the elevators were working. It was too hot, and there was no way I was carrying the stroller up even one flight of steps, let alone three. Thankfully, both elevators were active. As we waited on one, my phone rang. Picking it up from the cup holder, Jalen's new assigned contact name danced across the screen. I hit ignore without hesitation. He wanted to play courthouse games, I was going to ensure that all of our conversations consisted of texts only.

Yesterday, I was fuming about him having the audacity to even take it that far. This was the same guy who wanted to pencil in seeing his daughter rather than making real time. The same bitch ass nigga that was so hung up on me leaving him that he was letting it affect how he showed up as a parent. And I wasn't begging him to. Today, I was ready for whatever.

    HoAssNigga: I need to talk to you.

I read his text and sucked my teeth.

    Me: Any talking you want to do with me will be in front of the judge when we have our hearing in two months.

HoAssNigga: Listen, I can throw all that shit
out. I don't wanna be in nobody's court. You
know me, Mari. All I want is another chance to
raise our daughter together. Every kid deserves
that. Why do you insist on denying her that?

Me: Usually, my ho ass nigga radar is always on
point, so how I missed the mark with you beats
the fuck out of me. You don't get to start some
shit up and then think you're going to rescind it.
Keep that same energy you had when you took
yo ass up to them people court to file that
petition. You started some shit that I intend to
finish, Jalen. In the meantime, I'll have a set
schedule to you this week so that you're able to
see your daughter. Have the day you're
supposed to have.

The elevator doors opened just as I sent the text off. I knew
it wouldn't be long before Jalen texted back a response that
would go unread. I came from the *show a nigga tribe*. And I was
gonna do just that with him.

"Grandma, we're hereeee!" I announced as I pushed the door
open to GNani's.

"Awww, come in. Come in, GNani's baby," she replied with
the same excitement. "Turn the AC down, Mia."

"Oh, I didn't even know you were here," I said to Tamia as I
pulled the stroller inside, closing the door behind myself.

She hugged me, while GNani picked Amari up, completely
disregarding my existence.

"Dang, she act like she don't even see you," Tamia joked.

"That's what I'm saying."

"Haters gon' hate, Amari. Always remember that." GNani
blew me a kiss and walked over to the couch.

"That's your grandmother," Tamia said, shaking her head.

"**Our** grandmother."

"And don't y'all ever forget it, baby. What y'all doing over this way, Mari?"

"I wanted to get some air and figured we'd come over here to hang for a little."

"Ookay. Where's your third party?" she asked, situating Amari in her lap.

"My third party?"

"Don't try to play confused." Tamia called me out. "Where Melly Mel?"

I laughed. "Not Melly Mel. And he's working. Had a few clients lined up today."

"Alright now. My girl know the schedule and everything. Period!"

"You so damn animated." GNani chuckled. "So, when y'all make it official, Mari?"

I couldn't contain the smile that broke through. "And how do you know that we made things official?"

"Girl, you all but gave us that man's itinerary for the day. Men don't let women know their schedules unless they're important to them. Plus, we already had a conversation about you."

"Really?"

"Yep. And I gave him simple advice on how to deal with one of mine. Come correct or don't come at all."

Me and Tamia nodded. "Funny I told him the same thing. Told him to keep up the same energy."

"I love this for you!" Tamia exclaimed. "I love the glow. I'm loving your smile. I mean, you never gave pressed or stressed behind no man. But you look light. Almost like you don't have to think. And you know that's the typa shit I like. I wanna go through life like Stevie Wonder when I got a man."

Me and GNani cracked up laughing at Tamia standing and walking with her eyes closed.

"Mia, please. Something is wrong witchu. I still think, but in the event I experience brain fog, I feel that he'll be there to clear it up. Like, yesterday. I was so flustered about Amari's pediatrician being changed the day before her appointment. I felt like I was missing things from her diaper bag, while I was getting ready." I paused, going back to the moment that made my heart leap. "Why Melly had a checklist he made the night before? Like who does that?"

"A thinker," GNani answered. "A man who wants you or wants the best for you should be able to meet a need before you can express it. When there's a problem, have a solution. Correct you when you need correction. And lead you even when he knows you have the tools to lead yourself."

"A word," Tamia cosigned, sitting back down next to me.

"Once you feel like you gotta lead a nigga, that's when you leave a nigga," GNani added, and that hit home.

I thought about Jalen and exhaled. "Jalen had me served with custody paperwork yesterday."

"You surprised?" GNani asked, laying Amari down on the couch.

"Shit, I am," Tamia responded before me.

"I'm very surprised, GNani," I said, taking offense to her question.

"I'm not. Jalen didn't think you'd get tired at some point, baby. Which is why he trapped you with this baby." She pointed to Amari. "Only it's not a trap because you wanted her. Jalen don't want custody, Amariyah. He wants control. And for him, filing a petition is the start of that. I've never been a fan of his. But as your grandmother, I was cordial. And it's not my job to choose your man/future husband. I knew his ass was never it though."

"Wait a minute now, G," Tamia said. "You ain't like Ty either. And you weren't cordial. You made that known." Ty – or Tyron – was Tamia's ex that we all gave the cold shoulder to and for good reason.

"Mia, we all knew you was with that ugly, rude ass boy for his money. You didn't even like him."

There was a knock at the door, and GNani got up to answer it, while Tamia sat back quietly.

I snickered. "She ain't lying, Mia."

"I know," she agreed. "That's why I sat back and shut up. I ain't gon' argue when you right."

"Girlll." I laughed and paused, slowly turning my head toward the front door. I felt Melly as he entered.

"Here go your weekly blessings, G," he said, handing her her lotto tickets.

"Thank you, son. Bout to be rich rich."

With his signature smirk, Melly walked into the living room and went right to Amari. "Where the hand sanitizer at, shorty?" he asked me. "Wassup, Tamia?"

"What's going on, Melly? I see everybody ignoring my cousin today. Amari done took over forreal."

"I swear," I agreed with a smile.

Melly's eyes found mine, and he licked his lips. "Don't do that, Ma." He stepped back and leaned over me to kiss my forehead. Wanting more, I lifted my head and met his lips. "Can I get my baby now?"

"Mmhmm." I nodded. "Hand sanitizer on the side of the diaper bag."

We all watched as he gently picked her up from the couch and cradled her in his arms. Synchronized awww's came from both GNani and Tamia, making me laugh.

"There go my lil' mama," he cooed, swaying gently. "You missed me?"

Amari kicked and blew spit bubbles in response.

"Oh, while you're here, let me give you this bag, Mari," GNani let out before disappearing to the back of the apartment.

"Soooo, that lil' six-week shut down is over, huh?" Tamia clapped and danced in her seat. "And right around the time y'all made it official. All I'm saying is if y'all need the weekend to really solidify things, ya girl can babysit. Wassup?"

"I appreciate that, Tamia. But lil' mama gon' have to go where we go for a lil' bit longer. Mari gon' be quiet when I'm in there though, right, Ma?"

My face became flushed, and my clit thumped as I looked back up at him.

"You gon' be quiet, Ma?" Tamia repeated, and Melly laughed.

"Shut up, Mia. And I'm not answering that." I grinned.

"Okay, here it is." GNani returned with a Burberry bag. "I'm sorry, Melly. I done held onto this bag so long."

"It's cool, G. She should be able to fit it now."

"Awww, this is the gift," I said, pulling out two pairs of Burberry crib shoes.

"I didn't know what kinda clothes to get, so I went with shoes. You fuckin' wit em?" he asked.

"I love them."

"Yeah. You gon' be the flyest lil' mama," he said to Amari.

"Mannnnn, who is cuttin' onions?" Tamia had her head up, blinking.

Laughing, I put the shoes back in the bag and underneath the stroller.

"Did I interrupt something?" Melly asked the collective.

"No, baby," GNani responded. "If you came to collect your girls, we won't stop you."

"Wow. I told you we stopped by to hang with you."

"And I love you for that, boo. But your man wants to spend some time with you, so go head. And take her dramatic ass with you." She pointed to Tamia who laughed.

Placing Amari back in her stroller, we said our goodbyes and headed out the door.

"Teeny still has your car?"

"Yeah. I want you to take a ride with me. Well, technically, I'll be riding with you." He laughed. "But I wanna take you somewhere."

"Okay. Am I dressed for the occasion?" I gestured to my sundress and sandals.

"You look good, Ma. Perfect." He kissed my lips and pressed for the elevator.

"Wanna tell me where we going?"

"You'll see when we get there. There's somebody I want you to meet."

I wanted to ask more questions, but I was good with surprises, so I rolled with it. So long as I was in his presence, I was good.

10

MELLY

I manned the wheel of Amariyah's Audi as we drove along the freeway. The drive was quiet, more so because I was in my head about the destination. My chest was too full for words because what I was about to do was something I'd never had a chance to do with Paige. And it wasn't that we couldn't but because she didn't want to. Out of respect for her space at the time, I never expressed to her how much it bothered me or how it pushed me away from her. Even now, when I thought about it, it was another reason on the list of cons of us getting back together.

Amariyah stole glances at me, likely wondering if I would reveal where we were going at some point, but I said nothing. I just kept my eyes on the road with one hand rested on her thigh, giving it a reassuring rub every now and then. Turning down a long dirt road lined with old oak trees, she sat up straight, and her body tensed. Her breath hitched, leg jumping up and down when the cemetery came into view.

"My mother is buried here," she said quietly, her voice a mixture of memory and pain. "I haven't been back since my first trimester with Amari. I wanted to… but I was scared that my grief would be too much for me to have a healthy pregnancy. I didn't want the baby to feel that." Tears ran freely down her cheeks. "I… I just abandoned her."

I stopped the car, parking in the small lot. Turning off the ignition, I turned to her. "You didn't abandon her, Ma. You did what you felt was best at the time. You put Amari's needs in front of your own, just as I'm sure ya moms did for you countless times."

Wiping her face, she nodded. "What are we doing here?"

"There's someone I want you to meet."

Amariyah's eyes searched mine for a few seconds before she opened the car door and stepped out.

"You wanna take the stroller or carry her?" I asked, getting out of the car and opening the back door.

"Is she sleep?"

Pulling the door open, Amari stared up at me with big, alert eyes and her little fingers in her mouth. "She's up," I confirmed.

"Okay. We don't need the stroller."

I took her out of the car seat, while Amariyah grabbed the diaper bag. Holding her securely in one arm, I wrapped the other around Amariyah's neck, and we started up a small trail to get to the gravesite. Walking across the grass, I stopped at the second set of headstones.

Cimani Angel Jefferson
Our Princess On Earth. Our Angel In Heaven.
Sunrise 6/17/2024 Sunset 6/17/2024

Buried beneath a headstone with butterflies along the edges was my baby. I'd requested the butterflies to symbolize her flying up in Heaven somewhere freely.

"This is my baby girl. This is my Cimani." My shoulders dropped, and I felt myself getting choked up.

"Here, let me get her." Taking the baby from my arms, she

rubbed my back in a soothing manner and began speaking. "Hey, Cimani." She sniffled. "It's such an honor to meet you, beautiful. I'm Amariyah, and this is Amari. We didn't expect to meet you today, but I'm glad we did. I want you to know two things. One, you're in good company because my mommy is just a couple feet away from you. And two," she glanced up at me then back down at the tombstone, "we're going to make sure your father is in good company down here. He won't lack any love. We got him." Wrapping her arms around my waist, she squeezed me. I let the weight of her presence hold me still. "I promise," she declared.

Crouching down, I brushed what little debris I saw from the headstone. "I miss you, Cimani. And I hope I'm making you proud. Daddy got a woman now too. On some solid shit."

I heard Amariyah whisper, "Oh, my God," behind me while giggling.

"I needed her to meet you. Amari too. I love you so much. Daddy number one. Till the end of forever." Placing my hand on the headstone, I sent up a silent prayer. Standing, I reached for Amariyah's hand. "Come introduce me to your angel." Taking Amari from her, I gestured for her to walk forward. "I'll follow you."

She took slow, cautious steps over to her mother's headstone. Kneeling once she reached it, she pressed her palm gently to the headstone. There were no audible words at first. Then, as if she'd needed some kind of sign that it was okay to speak her thoughts, her phone rang. Pulling it out of the diaper bag, she answered it. By the pause, I knew it was her father calling. His timing couldn't have been any more perfect.

"Hey, Daddy. One second." She put the phone on speaker. **"Can you hear me?"**

"Yeah. And the birds too. What you up to?"

"I'm here at the cemetery with the baby and Melly."

"You took the baby to see your mama?" he asked, his voice heavy with emotion.

"Melly brought us to meet his daughter, Cimani. And to see Mommy. They're in the same cemetery, Daddy. A few feet away from each other."

There was a long pause.

"Is he there?"

"Yeah. He's here."

"How you doing, Prince?"

"I'm doing good. Real good, man. This was some stand up shit to do. I appreciate it. And I hope your princess is resting peacefully."

"Thanks, man."

"No doubt. Princess," he called out to Mari.

"Yes, Daddy."

"Let me say something to Mommy before I go."

"Okay, one sec." She placed the phone on top of the headstone. **"Go head."**

"We did a damn good job, Mama. I love you still."

I watched as new tears ran down Amariyah's face while fighting back my own. And I did not want to cry in front of my woman.

"I love you, Daddy."

"I love y'all too, Princess. I'm gonna call you tomorrow."

"Okay." Ending the call, she put the phone down. "Hey, Mommy. I hope you're not mad at me for staying away so long. I'm sure you know I gave you a beautiful granddaughter. GNani say she look just like you and act like me already. We're doing really good too. Oh, and that person you told me I'd find all those years ago… I found him. Thanks, my girl. I love you."

Standing, she stepped back so that she was at my side. My hand went to her waist. "We'll come visit them both twice a month. Together."

"Thank you, Jamel."

"Nah, thank you." I kissed her forehead, and we stood there a few minutes longer.

We both needed this moment of remembrance. And I'd admit that it felt good being able to experience another stage past my grief with someone by my side.

"How'd you know my mom was buried at that cemetery?" Amariyah asked as we laid cuddled up on the couch. Her back was pressed against my chest, while I held her close.

"GNani told me a couple days ago. We were talking about me wanting to take you to see Cimani. She asked where she was buried and confirmed your mom was buried there too. It didn't seem like a coincidence to me. It was meant for us to show up today and show them that somebody got us."

Turning to face me, her eyes glossed over. "What you shared with me today was something very special. A part of you that's so sacred. I don't know why you feel I deserved such an honor, but I'll never forget it."

Brushing her hair from her face, I kissed her lips. "Special people deserve to know other special people, Ma. Can you do something for me?"

"Mmhmm," she replied, pulling at my locs.

"Come wash my hair for me, so I can grab your booty while I act like I'm reaching for a towel."

Leaning back, she smirked. "You got me over here all emotional, and now you want me to wash your hair, so you can cop free feels?"

Nodding, I smirked. "Pretty much. We've bonded over the baby, food, and our careers. Now, we can bond over a retwist."

Rolling her eyes playfully, she got up. "We gon' be up all night. Let me go grab the stuff." I watched as she made her way to the back of the house, ass jiggling in her cotton shorts with each step she took. I had to readjust my hard on. Ass had a mind of its own forreal.

A few minutes later, we were in the kitchen. And I didn't have to fake like I was grabbing a towel to cop a feel. I just held onto that motherfucka the whole time. It was worth the cramp in my arm by the time she was done.

"Okay, step back so I can…"

Before she could finish her sentence, I threw my head back, splashing her with water.

"Boy!" She gasped, jumping back.

"What?" I faked innocence.

"Oh, you wanna play? Cause we can play." She inched toward the sink, and I followed her lead.

"You gon' wake up the baby, shorty."

She stopped and nodded. "You right. Here, dry your head." She pointed to the towel.

I reached for the towel, and at the same time, her slick ass grabbed the sprayer and tried to soak me with it, but I ducked just in time.

"Oh, yo' slick ass." Pulling her to me by her waist, I took the sprayer from her and dropped it in the sink.

She squealed, laughing loudly. "Okay, okay. You got it. We gon' wake the baby up." I let her pull away and stood frozen once she did.

"You ain't got no bra on?" I let out, mesmerized by how full her titties were.

She locked eyes with me with a smile tugging at her lips. "No."

"Remember that six-week cool down period ya cousin was talkin' bout? And that whole solidifying the relationship shit?

"Uh huh."

"Well, we bout to get into that."

Pulling my wife beater over my head, I tossed it to the side. I dropped my shorts and boxers without hesitation. Stroking my already semi hard dick to its full length, I closed the distance between us.

"Yeah. Go head and smile. I'ma bout to put it in your mouth."

Biting her bottom lip, she followed my lead, stripping out of her shirt and shorts. I pushed her body back against the sink and smashed my lips into hers while gripping two handfuls of her ass.

"Mmmm," she moaned into my mouth, while I spread her ass cheeks and slid a finger down the crack of her ass.

"You gon' have to gimme this pussy, Amariyah." Pulling my lips from hers, I latched onto her neck, sinking my teeth into it.

"Ahhhhhh," she let out, throwing her head back.

"I'ma have to tattoo my name on this shit, you hear me?" I smacked her ass hard, and she let out a soft whimper.

"Yesss," she cooed.

"You gotta do something for me first." Taking a break from her neck, I traced a trail with my tongue down to her titties. Cuffing the left one in my hand, I sucked her nipple into my mouth gently. I knew she was still breastfeeding, and I could taste a hint of her breastmilk as I sucked. I didn't give a fuck. Amari was gon' have to share these. "Amariyah."

"Ssss, yessss."

Releasing her titty, I put my hand around her neck and gave it a light squeeze before licking her lips. "You gotta let me touch the back of that throat, baby. A nigga been wanting to put it in your mouth for so long. Can I do that? Huh?" I kissed her. "Can I get in there?"

"Yes."

That single syllable hung in the air for a few seconds before she pushed me back and squatted in front of me. Wrapping her soft hands around my shaft, she stuck her pink tongue out and tapped my dick on it. I'd had my dick sucked plenty of times, but there was something about the passion and challenge in Amariyah's eyes as she did it that made me want to skeet down her throat. She bobbed her head slowly at first, saliva slipping out the sides of her mouth, confirming just how wet that motherfucka was.

Getting into a groove, she got real nasty with it. When it hit the back of her throat and I heard those gawking sounds, I was done.

"You so fucking nasty," I said, pumping in and out of her mouth. "Oooouuu, I'ma bout to suck on that clit so good. You gon' wish you gave a young nigga a chance sooner."

My words must've boosted her ego because she held on to my legs and sucked faster. "Mmmm, mmm." No words, just sounds. The sound of fuckin' Heaven.

"Shit, girl. You betta suck that dick. Goddamn! Ughh. I'ma bout to bust."

Pulling my dick out her mouth, she held her tongue out and milked my shit with her hands. I bust so hard my legs shook.

"Ooohhh, shit. Wait, wait." I grabbed at the counter for balance.

"I'm gonna go check on the baby," she said, standing and wiping her mouth.

"Oh, nah. You not bout to be running around telling your cousin you fucked my head up. We both bout to be walking around this bitch coo coo." Turning her around, I bent her over the sink and slid into her from behind.

"Ouuuu, shittt, Melly."

"I know, baby. The feeling is fucking mutual. Damn, this shit tight." Holding onto her waist, I dug into her slowly. "A nigga gon' have to die behind this pussy. I swear. This shit so warm."

She spread her own cheeks and threw that ass back on my dick, creaming each time she met my pelvis.

"You just gon' wet that dick up like that and not tell me you cumming, Ma?" Grabbing both of her hands so that they were locked behind her back, I drilled into her.

"Ahhhh, ahhhh. Shit, just like that!!!"

"Nah, hold it down fore you wake the baby." I dipped a little lower, so I could hit that spot, and she did that pussy squeeze shit.

"I'm cummin'," she shrieked.

"Shit, me too." Pulling out, I sprayed all over her ass. "Ahhhhhhhh."

Breathing hard, I managed to wet a piece of paper towel to wipe her off as best I could, then myself. Kissing her back, I pulled her into me. "Now, you can go check on the baby."

Putting my shorts and boxers back on, I laid my wet shirt out on a dining room chair.

"I'm gonna go change."

"Aight."

With all the rocking we were doing, I was surprised that Amari didn't wake up. She must've known her mommy needed her back cracked. I headed back into the living room, and before I could sit down, the doorbell rang.

"Can you grab the door?" she called out. "I think it's the food."

"Got it." Taking a $50 bill from my wallet, I went to the door. I opened it, and instead of it being a delivery guy on the other side of it, it was a dude that looked a few years older than me but still young. "Can I help you?"

"Help me? Nigga, who are you?"

Before I could reply, I could hear Amariyah behind me. "What are you doing here, Jalen?"

I glanced back to make sure she was in something decent, and when I saw that she was in pajama pants and a t-shirt, I nodded my approval before turning back to who I now knew was her bd.

"Who the fuc..." I didn't even let him finish before I stole on him, catching him off guard.

"Melly!" she yelled out, but I didn't stop swinging.

I was about to show this bitch ass nigga exactly who I was.

He swung back, a few hits connecting, but they were no match for what I was throwing. He tried to bear hug me and sweep me off my feet, but I was too quick, hitting him with two rights and a mean left that put him on his ass.

"Okay, Melly. Come on, bae. Please. That's enough." Amariyah pulled me back by my arm, while his bitch ass backed up to his car.

"Fuck you and that baby, Amariyah!" he hissed.

I went to break from her grasp, and she stopped me. "He ain't even worth it, Jamel. He's not."

With a bloody face and a bruised ego, he hopped in his car and sped off, almost side swiping her car that we'd parked on the street. Entering the house, we went separate ways – me to the bathroom to check my hands and her to the living room. Seeing the bruising on my knuckles pissed me off. Knowing that I hadn't been able to really do that nigga dirty pissed me off even more. Washing my hands, I dried them and walked back out to find her.

"He texted," she said, holding the screen out.

> HoAssNigga: While yo ass out here fucking on niggas and tryna play house, tell that nigga to take care of you and the baby. I dropped the custody case, so you ain't ever gotta worry bout me. When Amari is old enough, she'll come and find her real daddy.

My face scrunched up. "And that's the clown you gave that good ass pussy to? That's wild as fuck. But anyway, fuck that nigga. He ain't ever gotta worry bout my baby," I said with conviction. "So long as I got breath in my lungs, she'll never know what it's like not to have a father. Nigga thought he was sayin' something but ain't saying shit."

"I can't believe you were just out there fighting with him."

"Well, believe it. It was the time and place. Now, take all that off and come ride this dick. Cause I won the fight."

"Oh, my God." She giggled while standing to strip.

Taking my shorts and boxers off, I laid down on the couch, and she got on top of me. "Thank you again."

"You're welcome again."

I put my dick at her opening, and she slid down slowly. There was no place I'd rather be. Amariyah was now home.

11

AMARIYAH

It had been two weeks since the fight and two weeks since I'd seen or heard from Jalen. A part of me wanted to think he wasn't serious about basically saying fuck his child, but as the days went on, I realized that was exactly what it was. I guess I should've known when I called the courts a few days ago and confirmed that he had withdrawn the custody petition. There were no court appearances lingering over my head. Nothing pending in court. It was basically over. And while that door had shut, everything else in my life was flourishing.

My man signed a lease for his barber suite a week ago after successfully completing his classes to earn his business degree. Watching him work overtime to get the place to his liking in that week's time made me so proud. The only person I knew with drive that matched Melly's was my own. He was hell bent on building his own, and he did it. Not just for himself. But for his sisters, his aunt, and to show anyone that doubted his abilities that he was, in fact, that nigga.

Today was my first official day back behind the chair, and I was in the groove. One wouldn't know that I boo hoo cried earlier in the day when I dropped Amari off to Melly before coming in. She was only going to be with him for two hours before he dropped her off to GNani's to take a few clients. And even though he'd promised to FaceTime me every thirty minutes, I still didn't feel it was enough. Over my shenanigans, he walked me to my car, called me a crybaby, and sent me on my merry way.

We'd made a pact that we would work around each other so that we wouldn't have to lean on family as much. Together, we were going to figure it out. Between reminder texts about schedules, daily check-ins, and even post-it reminders, we were going to work as a team. And I loved that Melly was continuing to give everything 110%. My man wasn't half stepping. My YN was giving big dawg in every sense of the word.

"Hey, Amariyah. Do you think I can catch a ride with you when you leave?" Teeny asked from her station.

"Of course, boo. I'm going by your brother's to pick up Amari, then I can drop you home."

"Okay, cool."

The door chimed, and I looked up just as Toni walked in. She was the last person I expected to see at my place of business.

"Welcome to Serenity. Do you have an appointment today?"

"I got it, Mariah," I said, walking over. "Thank you. You can step outside with me, Toni."

Like a child knowing they were about to be chastised, her shoulders dropped, and she walked outside. "I'm sorry to have come up to your place of business, but I couldn't get you on the phone."

"Thanks for letting me know my blocking feature works."

Her mouth opened then closed then opened again. "I wanted to apologize for the role I played in what happened between you and Jalen. We were wrong. I was wrong. I overstepped in ways I shouldn't have."

"Before I dissect that bullshit apology of yours, let's be clear on a thing. First, you didn't happen to me and Jalen. Jalen happened to me and Jalen. I left him before I found out about the two of you. So, don't go giving yourself the credit like you broke something up. Two, it's a little too late for apologies that ain't gon' go past this parking lot. I'm cool on you, been cool on Jalen. And there's only two things keeping me off your ass right now. The fact that I've been on my feet the last six hours in these cute ass shoes and I'm a professional. Now, should you see me out in Whole Foods and I have on my Asics, I suggest you act like you don't see me cause, bitch, I'ma have you calling on the ancestors. You have a blessed day, Toni."

Leaving my words to marinate, I went back into the shop. The best thing for her to do was take heed because she'd gotten off easy. Another scene in the Jalen chapter closed.

When we made it to Melly's suite, there was a client walking out as we entered.

"Amari!" Teeny exclaimed, picking her up from the portable bassinet Melly had set up against the wall. "Oh, my God. When you got her this shirt?" She turned her around, and I laughed.

"My daddy is the dopest barber ever," I read the words on the shirt out loud and kissed her cheeks. "That was not in the bag this morning," I said, walking over to kiss him.

"I know. I had it made. My client's wife has a printing shop. She dropped it off today."

"This is so cute," Teeny complimented.

I sat down in the barber chair. "How was she today?"

"Perfect. The same way she is any other day," he replied,

pulling off his gloves. "She may need to be here more often. They seem to tip more."

"You not bout to use my baby for clout." I laughed.

"Maannnn, please."

"Guess who came by my shop today?"

"Who?" he asked, pulling me up from the chair and sitting me down on his lap.

"Toni."

"Erykah Badu? Fuck she want?"

"To apologize."

"Oh." He kissed my exposed shoulder. "You told her beat her feet?"

"No. I told her that if I caught her in the grocery store and I had on my Asics that I was gon' tap that ass."

"Shiiiddd, I like that energy better."

"I know you do." I giggled.

"Time and place."

"That's right, baby."

Amari began to fuss and give Teeny a hard time. "Hungry, are we?" she asked, handing her to me. Only the fussing didn't stop.

"Gimme my baby," Melly requested with his arms out. "She just ate." I put her in his arms, and she was all smiles.

"He is not all that," Teeny said, and I laughed.

I got up and looked at the two of them – the daughter I'd birthed and the man who showed up and was continuing to show up – and felt overwhelming gratitude.

"You aight?" he questioned.

"Yes. I love you."

Smirking, he winked. "I know you fuck wit a young nigga. I love you too."

The End

AHT! AHT! FINE, SHII. DON'T START THAT. Y'ALL ALREADY KNOW HOW THIS WORKS. I AIN'T GOT NO MO' FOR THESE CHARACTERS. DIS IT... DIS ALL! LOVE YOU. MEAN IT.

DID YOU ENJOY?

Did you enjoy the read?
Let us know how much by leaving us a
review on Amazon and Goodreads.

His Hood Love Gave Me Life 2

My Thug, My Sanctuary

Thug Kisses For Christmas

For The Love Of My Savage

Charge It To The Game

Charge It To The Game 2

Charge It To The Game 3

Charge It To The Game 2

Charge It To The Game 3

A Summer To Remember With My Hitta

Snatched Up By A Hitta

Santa Sent Me A Real One For Christmas

Wet Dreams On Lockdown: The Unit Manager

Thug Me The Right Way 2

Thug Me The Right Way 3

Seizing A Gangsta's Heart For The Summer

Yours For The Taking

Wrapped Up In A Hitta's Love For Christmas

By **Nai**

A Set Up For Revenge

A Set Up For Revenge 2

Wet Dreams On Lockdown: The Librarian

By **Ashley Williams**

Trickin' On A Heaux For Christmas

Homie Hoppin' For The Holidays

Wet Dreams On Lockdown: The Female C.O

Letters Of His Love

By **Telia Teanna**

The State's Witness

The State's Witness 2

The State's Witness 3

This Time Won't You Save Me

This Time Won't You Save Me 2

His Summer Side Piece

A Holiday Heist

Healing The Heart Of A Detroit Gangsta

Summer Vows With A Detroit Gangsta

The Promissory

By **Kyiris Ashley**

Stuck In The Trenches

Stuck In The Trenches 2

By **Huff Tha Great**

Melted The Heart Of A Menace

Wet Dreams On Lockdown: Lieutenant Grace

By **P. Wise**

Merry Trapmas

By **Mia Sky**

Thug Me The Right Way

By **DiamondATL & Nai**

Wet Dreams On Lockdown: The Counselor

By **Paris Iman**

Wet Dreams On Lockdown: The Male C.O

By **Tamyra Griffin**

Wet Dreams On Lockdown: The Captain

By **TN Jones**

Wet Dreams On Lockdown: The Warden

By **Shawnice**

Atlantastan

Atlantastan 2

By **Chris Green**

IN The Streetz

IN The Streetz 2

IN The Streetz 3

IN The Streetz 4

IN The Streetz 5

By **Tron Hill**

Hittin' Licks For The Holidays: New York

Bandemic

By **Freshh Moneyy**

Coming Soon From
URBAN AINT DEAD

Drill
The Hottest Summer Ever 2
THE G-CODE
Tales 4rm Da Dale 2
How To Build Your Credit From Prison
By **Elijah R. Freeman**

Despite The Odds 3
By **Juhnell Morgan**

A Felon's Promise
By **Nai**

The Promissory 2
By **Kyiris Ashley**

Atlantastan 3
By **Chris Green**

IN The Streetz 6
By **Tron Hill**

Bandemic 2
By Freshh Moneyy